The Virgin Billionaire

Switched at Marriage, Episode 2

Gina Robinson

Gina Robinson
SEATTLE, WASHINGTON

The Virgin Billionaire, Switched at Marriage 2/ Gina Robinson. — 1st ed.
ISBN 978-0692442777

For Jeff

CHAPTER ONE

Kayla

When staring into the eyes of a woman who is in love with your husband, you don't blink. You don't back down. And you absolutely do *not* let your shock show.

I was perched above Justin. In his lap, kissing him on the sofa. Trying not to let the tickle of his beard distract me. Facing her. He had his back to her. And she, the other woman, the assistant, was standing in the entryway to his penthouse. Holding a cleaner's bag. In a circle of sunshine from all those windows, as if she were an avenging angel come to rescue him. And deliver his dry cleaning. All light and goodness and righteous indignation. But whom was she saving him from? Me? *I* was the rescuer here. The good guy. Girl. Whatever.

And evidently I was doing a superb job of selling this marriage of convenience as the real deal. Because her eyes flashed daggers. Until that moment, I hadn't understood how eyes could do that. But right now, if she'd had a knife, I would have bet money she would have thrown it at me. Maybe not to kill me. Just to scare me off Justin's lap. But you never can tell how far a woman scorned will go.

I wanted to laugh. I wanted to tell her she shouldn't be jealous. That I wasn't in love with him. That I was just doing a friend a favor. If she could hold on for a year...

But under the terms of our marriage contract—wow, that sounded old-fashioned, like something from the Dark Ages—I couldn't disclose the terms of our marriage. As in how it wasn't for love. But, in the meantime, I would be damned if I shared him. It was a matter of pride. And it was a matter of me and authenticity. No one who knew me would buy me letting another girl in on my territory. *Sorry, Ophelia. You'll have to wait your turn.*

Justin had his hands on my hips. They froze in place. And went suddenly cold, like ice cubes gripping me. He had to crane backward to see her. "Ophie, what are you doing here?"

"You weren't answering your phone." Her words were heavy with accusation. She held up the dry cleaning. "Did you forget? You asked me to pick up your clothes for tonight. We have a function to attend together this evening. The EIEIO meeting. It's your big night, remember?"

EIEIO meeting? As far as I knew, Justin wasn't into farming or nursery rhymes. I wasn't getting the association. The Dead Nursery Rhymes Society? What was EIEIO?

And secondly, "function to attend together" was clearly code for "date." She thought she still had a date with my new bridegroom? On my supposed honeymoon? After our nuptials had been splashed all over the news? Oh, no way, honey. Not even. I had my pride. And my cool ten million to earn and protect. But at least that explained the dagger-shooting eyes.

Crap, I thought, as an almost frivolous afterthought. She did all that personal stuff for him, too. More like a personal assistant than an administrative assistant. She obviously let the lines blur into evening functions. And liked it. I wondered whether she would insist on picking out my anniversary present, too. Shudder. Oh, that's right—we weren't going to have an anniversary. But until then...

I slid off Justin's lap onto my feet and gave her my most innocent, sickeningly sweet smile. Yes, I really laid it on thick. Acting as naïve as a newborn Pomsky puppy as Data barked at my feet.

I scooped her up and took a step toward Ophie, extending my hand with that big smile plastered on. Acting like the ditzy blond that Ophie, in her tech girl way, looked down on and expected. "You must be Justin's assistant! Thanks so much for picking up his"—I stared at the cleaner's bag, trying to get a clue to the contents—"suit for tonight. I'm so excited to be making my public debut as his wife at the EIEIO meeting!"

Justin didn't have to be a secret agent to decode that one—*I* was going with him.

Somebody hand me my putty knife and my trowel, because I was laying it on and I wasn't done yet. "We haven't met. I'm Jus' new bride, Kayla." I giggled. Yes, giggled for effect as I took her limp hand and shook it. "You've probably seen me on the news."

Justin was on his feet now, trying to come between us, belatedly doing damage control. Poor Jus. I was pulling his chain as I stroked Data's soft fur and reached out for the dry cleaning. "I'll take that."

"Ophie, thanks." Justin shot between us. "I hadn't forgotten."

I waited, impatiently amused, to be honest, to see what he would do in his first official act as husband. Would he take back Ophie's plus-one for this big occasion? Or let her tag along as a fifth wheel? I intentionally hadn't cut dear Ophelia out of tonight's action. Giving him just enough wiggle room to hang himself if he wanted to keep her. Or needed her assistance for some reason. But it was clear I would be the girl hanging on his arm. That's what I was being paid for, after all.

"It's been a hell of a day," Justin said to her. "You deserve a night off. Take it. Kayla can handle the official meet-and-greet duties tonight." He put just the right amount of appreciation for her in his tone.

Impressive, I thought as I set Data down. And looked away before my smirk got out of hand. Which sounded heartless of me, but wasn't really. I had a heart that had recently been broken, too. I didn't want to see her crestfallen look. And I was afraid I would lose it by laughing at the absurdity of everything. And of course she wouldn't understand.

"If that's what you want," she said, sounding as if it was the last thing *she* wanted. "I'll have my hands full dealing with the media circus, anyway. We need to make an official announcement to the press before the stockholders and investors get nervous. Riggins will be on our case. Any idea what you'd like me to say?"

I was pulling the plastic bag up on Justin's suit to get a better look at it. And was being unpleasantly surprised in the process. This was definitely a case of less was best. It was...awful. The bag actually enhanced the suit's appearance. I inwardly sighed. And might have made some silent oaths about fashion-blind billionaires.

"It's already done," I said without looking at Ophelia. "I wrote a release and sent it to the communications team just before you arrived. It should be posted on Jus' social media and as an official statement, already released to the press as we speak. Who picked this out?"

"Ophie did," Justin said.

Damn, damn, damn! And she works for Flashionista, too? Unbelievable. Why doesn't he let one of his merch buyers dress him?

"Oh." I looked at her. When our eyes met, those daggers were back in hers. In addition to acing her out of a fabulous evening at an exciting EIEIO meeting and stealing her man, I'd just done her job. And she must have sensed I was flirting with bashing her sense of taste, style, and fashion. I smiled like we were besties, true blue, deep blue friends. Killing people with kindness was my particular specialty. "It's nice."

A smug look of satisfaction crossed her face. Like she was saying, *Yes, I buy his clothes. I know him better than you do. He belongs with me.*

"Everything's under control," Justin said. "Take the night off and relax for once." He laughed as if relaxing was a rare occurrence.

"Your speech?" she said.

"Written. Short and to the point." He paused. "Is there anything else that's urgent? If not, we'll catch up at the office tomorrow." He put his hand on her shoulder. Beneath all that fur on his face, he looked genuinely sympathetic. That's the thing about Justin. He was a considerate guy.

Which meant he was totally *not* my type. As a husband, anyway.

He showed her to the door. They paused, talking in low voices for a moment while I pretended to ignore them and be absolutely enthralled by that hideous suit. Just when I'd memorized nearly every horrible thread of that rag, she left. I tossed it carelessly over the nearest chair, eager to be rid of it.

"You're going to have to take away her key or code or whatever gets her in here. We can't afford to have her walk in on us and overhear something she shouldn't." I turned to face him. "I'll need my own key."

"Yes, you're right." He looked miserable, like he didn't relish telling her.

"Jus." I felt bad for him. I hugged him. Just slid into his arms. Without my shoes on, my head tucked nicely beneath his chin. It would have fit better if not for those long, tickling beard hairs hanging down. I pressed my head to his chest and listened to the wild beating of his heart. "You can give it back to her in a year. If you want to. Until then it's safer for us if she doesn't have such easy access."

The hammering of his heart became a full-out battering.

I looked up at him and had to blow the beard out of my face and take a step back. "Is something going on between you and her?"

He shook his head. "No. Why?"

He was too nonchalant to be completely believable. I studied him. I was usually pretty good at reading faces and sniffing out liars. I was going to have to learn his tell. *Everyone* had one. In the meantime, I thought he was fooling himself.

"That's not what *she* thinks. She's madly in love with you."

He looked startled and froze. As if he either didn't believe me or I'd found him out.

"EIEIO?" I was still in his arms, looking up at him.

"And on his farm he had a cow." Justin's eyes danced as he looked down at me.

I still wasn't used to him being so tall. And towering over me.

"I know. We get teased all the time. It stands for the Entrepreneurs, Inventors, and Engineers International Organization." His arms were locked around my waist as if he didn't want to let me go.

I should have stepped away. We were lingering too long for mere friends. But I didn't. Then again, we were in our honeymoon phase. I pursed my lips and tried not to laugh. "Clearly, you should have let some marketers in. And not just because you need a consonant in your organization name. I hope it never makes it as a *Wheel of Fortune* clue. Without the acronym, it's kind of bland and nondescript. This is the local chapter, I take it?"

He laughed. "The name's innocuous enough. Local chapter?" He frowned as if he was puzzled by my question.

"International?"

"Oh, yeah. That. We have a Canadian member. From BC. Vancouver. She comes down to the meetings. They couldn't exclude her in the title."

"I see," I said, when I didn't. "What does it do and why is this an honor?"

"Does this help? The nickname is the Jet City Billionaires' Club. But that sounds too pretentious." His lips curled into an adorable smile.

"Oh," I said. "Now I see why Ophie was disappointed you took back her invitation. Who wouldn't want to hang with a bunch of billionaires? How many are there?"

"It's a small group," he said, looking incredibly proud. "There are only forty-six billionaires under forty in the entire country."

"Yes, but you're including Canadian billionaires in your group."

"Doesn't up the number much."

"All these billionaires are young, then?" Some girls would say, *Yummy!* Happy, happy hunting grounds. And rub their hands together. But not me, obviously. I was a married woman now, though I sure didn't feel like one.

"Not all. A fair share." He was still amused by me.

"And single?"

"A couple of them."

"Hmmm...no wonder Ophelia was bummed about not being able to go. Especially now that her best prospect got away."

He squeezed me hard and suddenly so that I let out a squeak that made us both laugh.

"And you're giving a speech to them? As your adoring wife, I'm so incredibly proud!" I gave him a playful punch in the arm. "I'll have to remember to bring some tissues and wear waterproof mascara." I thought I might be getting a kink in my neck from staring up at him and faking a look of complete wifely adoration. Actually, I wasn't faking as much as I'd expected. I *was* impressed.

He shrugged. "Yeah, sort of. An acceptance speech. I'm being inducted as their youngest member. *Ever.*" He was so adorable when he was trying not to look completely, absolutely proud of himself. He tilted his head as if he was angling for another kiss.

"Hence the special suit." I glanced away. Not the smoothest maneuver to avoid a kiss and hurt feelings, but whatever. I tried not to sound as sarcastic about the suit as I felt.

As the implication of the importance of this event hit me, so did a wave of panic. This was really a *big* deal. I pulled away from him so suddenly I left him with his lips hanging in bare air.

"Oh my gosh!" I said. "What time? Where? And what's the dress?"

He recovered quickly and even managed to look amused by my sudden case of nerves. "Seven. At an undisclosed location. Business casual."

"There's barely time. We have too much to do. And I have nothing to wear. Where's my fairy godmother when I need her?" I didn't bother questioning him about the undisclosed location. Time for that later.

"This is a *big* deal. You're planning to wear a suit. You didn't even wear a suit to our potential divorce. Or our wedding. As far as I can tell." I glanced down at my skirt. "I can't wear these...these...divorcing clothes! I need something...*stunning*. Something befitting the wife of the youngest member ever to be welcomed into the club."

"You look great, Kay. You always do." The light in his eyes confirmed he meant it.

"You're too sweet, Jus. That's your problem." I smiled at him. I obviously had different standards. "I'm not dressed like a trophy wife. That *is* why you 'married' me, right? To be your arm candy." I grinned at him. "Crap. With your money, you could have had a supermodel. For much cheaper."

He grinned back. "I could have? Damn that billionaire-marrying identity thief."

I laughed. "We'll take our revenge on her soon enough." I put a finger to my chin, hamming it up. "On second thought. Not too soon. I owe her my fortune." I held out my hand. "And now, the first lesson in being a sugar daddy husband—credit card, please. I have work to do."

He hesitated.

I shook my hand impatiently. "It's not just for me. Fork it over." I pointed to that god-awful suit that I'd thrown over a chair. "I can't have you wearing—" I caught myself in time. There was no need to be cruel. "—a suit another woman picked out." A woman with no taste. "What's your size?"

"Forty-two long. There's no time. It will need to be tailored."

"You're full of objections." I glanced at my watch. Two o'clock. There was just time. If fate cooperated and my friend Allie was working today. I gave him the old up-and-down appraisal. Forty-two long looked about right. Slim, European cut. I was good at eye-balling sizes. "Your money talks, sweetie. Time to make it sing."

He pulled his wallet out of his pocket and removed a credit card.

As he held the platinum card out to me, I shook my head and laughed playfully. "Nice try."

His eyes were dancing, too. He knew full well what he was doing. Trying to pass off a mere platinum card!

I went up on tiptoe and cooed in his ear. "Hand over the black one, baby."

"Are you going to make it worth my while?"

"Credit for sex? I don't think so. I'm not a prostitute," I said, still laughing. "But I *will* make you into a billionaire Adonis."

"Promises, promises. You do see me?" He gestured toward himself, making a sweeping motion over his body. "This is the raw material you have to work with."

"I see. Better than you think. You're full of potential." I kept my hand out until he handed me the appropriate black card. "I'll need a tailor's tape."

He gave me a blank look.

"A tape measure? Never mind. I think I have one in my bag."

He arched one eyebrow in a look of mock shock. "You carry a tape measure around for fun?"

"Yeah, sure. In case I'm ever on *Let's Make a Deal.*" I laughed. "Duh. I'm a merch buyer in the fashion industry. It's a tool of the trade."

Not so much in the tighty whitey trade. But whatever. I grabbed my bag and dug it out. Within minutes I had his measurements, including his inseam. I was sure he'd held his breath as I got close to the boys. His discomfort as I ran my hand up his leg had been cute and adorable again. I teased him by running my fingers dangerously close, just for fun. Guys were so *easy.*

Data ran around our feet, trying to get our attention. But I was too distracted with thoughts of how much I had to do to pay much attention to her.

Jus picked her up as I grabbed my phone, plunked onto the sofa, and called my friend and former classmate, Allie. She worked as a sales associate at my favorite department store. At the nearest store to Justin's penthouse. Just a few blocks away, actually. A sales associate was the first step toward becoming a merch buyer. Until this afternoon, I'd envied her position and probable career trajectory. Who wouldn't? My trajectory had been decidedly downward. You can be envious *and* happy for a friend at the same time. I wanted her to get what she wanted. I just wanted mine, too.

"Well if it isn't the billionaire's bride. And I'm on the call list! Woo-hoo! I rate! I know a billionaire!" Allie was always so reassuring and bubbly. And genuinely happy for others.

"Hey to you, too!" I glanced at Jus. How many billions *did* he have? Yet another thing I should know as his wife. I wasn't going to be one of those women who has no idea how much her husband makes and where he hides his money. As if that mattered in our case. As long as he had the ten million he promised me.

But this was a community property state. So, worst case, I would have been a half-billionaire if I'd really married him under normal circumstances without the postnup. If he had more than two, I could have been a billionaire in my own right. *Don't get greedy, Lala!* But I made a mental note to find out.

"Best wishes, girl! Where are you registered? Neiman Marcus?" Allie laughed as if being registered, period, was a joke. How many elopers register? "What *do* you get a billionaire? Diamond-studded washcloths?"

"Trimmed in platinum." I laughed. "Your best wishes are present enough."

Her answering laugh was musical. "Isn't that sweet? You know I'm going to have to hit you up for money now, right? Isn't that what friends do when you become fabulously wealthy?"

"I hope not! You still owe me a twenty from two weeks ago."

"The deal was I was going to pick up lunch next time. I think that's off. The check's always yours from now on."

"Says you!" I teased back.

"We are so going to have to throw you a belated bachelorette party! We'll get the gang and some of your sorority sisters together."

"Sounds fabulous!" But I had a prickle of fear that despite her jesting, our relationship had subtly changed. I was the rich girl now.

"I want to hear the story—all the details of this whirlwind courtship. Justin Green? Really?"

Next to me, Justin shrugged as if he was getting used to it.

"I will. I promise. But I can't talk now."

"Oh, right. You probably have a million people to call. Or maybe a billion!"

"Haha," I said, smiling. "Actually, I'm on a mission. We'll get together and I'll fill you in on all the details later. Are you at work?"

"Yeah. Sadly."

"Not sadly at all! It's your lucky day. Being a billion-aire's bride's friend has its perks. How would you like to earn a fat commission? And get the scoop you can sell to the media about billionaire Justin's first big event out with his new bride?"

"I'm all in and all ears."

"Excellent. I need a personal shopper's complete attention for an hour or so. And someone to personally manage a tailor. Can you clear it with your boss?"

"To work for a billionairess? Are you kidding? Do you even need to ask?"

"I would run over there myself if I weren't afraid of being mobbed and recognized. I need a few things." I needed more than a *few* things. "They have to be delivered to Jus' penthouse ASAP. Do you still have that stunning pink dress we were eying last week?"

"Oh, yeah. And something even better that would look great on you. It just came in. What are we shooting for? Evening wear?"

"Smoking hot business casual. For evening. Nothing too new money. Nothing trampy or trashy. Something elegant. But with definite eye candy appeal. I'll need all the accessories, too—shoes, purse, makeup, foundations. You know my size?"

She laughed, knowing I was teasing. Of course she knew my size. It was the same as hers. We borrowed each other's clothes all the time.

"Grab a pen and paper. I have a long list of menswear I need, too."

I heard rustling, like she was looking for the pen.

"Got it!" she said. "Rattle on."

While Justin looked on in presumed horror, I gave Allie his measurements and ordered everything—suit, dress shirt, belt, socks, and shoes for him, detailing the look I was going for and the designer brands I thought would suit him.

"Wait! Is this for Justin? It all sounds, how to put this nicely, too big. Are you sure you have the right sizes?"

"He's grown since college," I said.

"He must have grown a lot. This inseam measurement is for a guy who's at least six feet. He doesn't look that tall on the news."

"He is. Trust me." I winked at him. "You know that shaving supplies boutique in the mall?"

"Yeah."

"I need you to run there, too. I don't think you have all the supplies I need in store."

"No problem. Anything for our richest customer." She laughed again. "What do you need?"

"Beard-trimming scissors, razors..." I glanced at Justin. He'd gone completely still. I whispered into the phone, "Beard oil. Hair clippers..."

He turned away and wandered off as if he couldn't bear to listen any longer. *A deal is a deal, Jus.*

"I'll call it in at the shop and pay for it. All you need to do is pick it up. And you know that Prada purse you've been lusting after?" I said at last. "Pick it up for yourself."

When she gasped, I laughed. "Told you! It's your lucky day."

CHAPTER TWO

Justin

An hour later, I was settled into a chair in the kitchen with a barber's cape wrapped around me. And Kayla poised over me with hair clippers and scissors in hand looking like the Barber of Seville. I don't know that she actually looked like the Barber of Seville so much as that was the only name of a famous barber I could think of while I was distracted by her. And that particular opera featured a couple with equally ridiculous marital/fake marital problems as mine. As far as I could remember from my ninth-grade fieldtrip to the opera, anyway.

Unlike most of my class, I'd understood the Italian. But I'd only been ten. So you could forgive my fidgety lapse of inattention to the plotline and actual performance. The story wasn't appealing to a boy that age. Even then, I was more into indie music than opera and foppishly dressed characters.

Speaking of which, getting my hair cut in the kitchen made me feel like a boy again. I swallowed hard as she studied my face with the intensity of an artist, wishing she saw what I wanted her to see—the real me. The guy who wasn't at all unhappy about ending up married to her.

"You've really filled out, Jus." Her voice was soft, sweet, and gentle.

Kay had never hurt me. Intentionally. Though she'd killed me a million times by loving that douche Eric instead of me. I'd showed him. I had the girl. Formerly his girl.

"I think you might have good bone structure. It's hard to tell exactly beneath all that hair." She snipped the scissors in the air for emphasis.

She was reveling in her power, testing it. Teasing. Flirting, I hoped. How the hell does a guy take a wife and only get to hope she's flirting with him?

I leaned away from her. "Who are you? Edward Scissorhands?"

"That's Edwardina to you."

Why did her smile make me so damned happy? I wanted to laugh and take her in my arms. I wanted her to see this wasn't fake to me. Fashion was her thing. I forgave her that. Thought it was awesome she wanted to look nice and make me proud. I wanted her to be eye candy and turn every head at the club meeting, knowing she was coming home with me. I didn't give a damn how *I* looked. Probably never would.

I liked the beard. More than I cared to admit. I would never say, but I hid behind it, behind its statement of manliness. I'd been on the wrong end of too many beatings not to. Behind the cover of my beard I was unreadable. The wolverine. Fierce. If she shaved it off, would I grow weak like Samson? Was she my Delilah? How the hell did I know?

"My talking money couldn't convince a hair stylist to come to the penthouse?" I probably should have pleaded for my beard's life. But it seemed futile. The woman drove a hard bargain. And I let her. Because she owned my heart.

"Don't worry." She brushed my concern aside with a laugh and a wave of her hand. "I'm a hair-cutting savant. I've been cutting hair since I was toddler. My mom says I'm the only two-year-old she's ever heard about who looked better *after* I took scissors to my own hair. She knew then I had genius." Her smile was infectious.

"In college, I cut all my sorority sisters' hair. I could have gone to beauty school. But, alas, I chose a college degree instead. And the world lost a great talent." She snipped the scissors again, slicing bare air and glancing at a picture on her phone that she refused to show me. Sighing, she leaned over and felt my face. "Crap, you grow a mean beard."

"It's awesome. Virile. Manly." I raised one eyebrow, hoping to get her to agree. Wanting her to see for herself I wasn't a boy anymore.

She stroked my beard and pursed her lips, looking deep into my eyes. "You really love this big, bushy thing?"

"I do."

"Poor, misguided baby." She leaned in so close, I thought for a minute she was going to kiss me again. I held still, unwilling to risk another rejection. Knowing I couldn't take another round of her passionate kisses without taking her. I was inexperienced. But I wasn't dead.

"Hmmmm..." she said, her face inches from mine. "Hair or beard first?" She squinted in thought and plugged in her hair clippers while I eyed that fine, shapely butt of hers. "Hair it is. If I screw up, we can always shave your head, too."

"What!" I played to her game, pretending to be ready to bolt.

"Nice try. But I know you're not scared." She grinned and turned businesslike. "FYI, I like to buzz dry hair. We'll shampoo after to get rid of all the annoying hair schnitzels."

"Hair schnitzels?"

"What? Isn't that what everyone calls them?"

"Ah, no."

"Well, too bad. That's what Mom always called them." She plugged her phone into a portable speaker I kept in the kitchen. "I work better to music."

I rolled my eyes, hoping for the best as One Direction blasted out and she began dancing and teasing me with the clippers. "A snip snip here. A snip snip there. Here a snip. There a snip. Everywhere a snip snip."

"I'm never going to hear the end of EIEIO, am I?"

She grinned and started humming to One Direction while I sat silent, enjoying the show, and the sound of her voice while she worked. Watching her breasts jiggle in my face and becoming horny as hell. Admiring the way she danced and moved as she wielded her clippers. She had a sweet singing voice.

This is absolutely insane. I'm married to the girl of my fantasies. And I promised not to touch her. What was I thinking?

There is only so much torture a guy can take.

She was running the comb through my bangs, brushing my hair back as she wielded her scissors, ready to cut, when she paused and gently touched my hairline. "You have a scar here. The hair doesn't grow in it. I've never noticed it before. What happened?"

"Childhood accident. The usual stuff. Guys horse-playing around."

"Oh."

The sympathetic look in her eyes almost killed me. It was almost as if she realized I was lying.

"Do you always wear your hair to cover it?"

Damn, if she kept touching me like that I was going to lose it. "Usually, yes." My voice was tighter than I intended.

She bit her lip like she was thinking, and nodded. But that damned sympathy was in her eyes. "I'll just hide it, then."

She went back to work. At last, she brushed my neck off with the world's softest brush. Pure sable hair, she told me. And stepped back to admire her work. She bit her lip in that beautiful way that turned me on and made me ache to kiss her. And squinted as if looking for imperfections and errant schnitzels or whatever the hell she called them. At last, she smiled. "Perfect. To the sink with you for a shampoo."

She dusted the hair off me—why the hell was her touch so tantalizing?—and swept up while I positioned my chair with its back to the kitchen sink and tried to get a glimpse of myself in the stainless steel toaster. I made a mental note to have the maid polish it to a mirror-quality sheen.

"Are you trying to peek?" Kayla came flying to me with a bottle of shampoo in her hand. "Cheater!"

I smiled at her. I couldn't stop smiling. Things were working out better than I'd hoped. I didn't need a supermodel. I had the hottest date around.

She ran the water and tested it with her fingers with as much concern as if she were testing the water for a baby's bath. Then she positioned my head beneath the faucet and wet my hair before massaging in sweet-smelling shampoo.

The feel of her fingers in my hair both turned me on and was tantalizingly relaxing. I could fall asleep with her stroking me like that and have a nice erotic dream in the process. "You're good with your hands."

She smiled as she rinsed my hair. "That's what they tell me."

"Who are *they*?" I pictured her cutting that asshole Eric's hair and lovingly massaging his scalp. And wanted to take him down. Hack his accounts and show him what a shitty bastard he was.

"Everyone. I actually took a class in scalp massage."
She laughed again and began massaging conditioner,
also good-smelling stuff, into my hair. "Now, we'll let
that sit for a few minutes. Then we'll blow-dry and
style. And work on the beard." She had an evil, teasing
glint in her eyes as she leaned over me. I was at her
mercy. As I had been since the first time I saw her.

"You had to ruin the mood," I teased.

She laughed and moved out of my line of sight,
humming again to her music. "You know, Jus. I was
thinking, if we're going to make this marriage look believable, we're going to need the media on our side."

My head was tipped back in the sink. I tried to sit up
just as she reappeared and pushed me back down,
phone in hand. "I avoid the media as a matter of poli-
cy."

"Hmmmm," she murmured. "I know. But policies
can be changed." She stared at the screen of her phone,
distracted, and began typing wildly with her thumbs.
Damn she was fast.

"What are you doing?" I tipped my head up.

"Updating my status and informing the world, and
the media, who is certainly following my social media
feeds now, that my wonderful new husband is taking
me out tonight to show me off to his powerful, rich
friends. And OMG! I can hardly wait." She laughed.

She was not an OMG type girl. Kayla played the
bubble-headed blond when it suited her. But beneath
the façade, she wielded a high IQ.

"No!" I reached for her and the phone.

She pushed me back down with the palm of her hand. "Too late! Prepare for a photo op when we leave." She leaned over me and smiled into my eyes. "I have a com minor. You'll thank me later. Believe me."

"Great," I said. "I've created a monster. You've gone all Kardashian on me."

She whispered into my ear as she turned the water back on. "Do you want to sell this or not?"

I wanted her to stay. "You're the one with the social sense."

"Exactly. You're in capable hands." She grabbed the spray nozzle from the sink and rinsed the conditioner out of my hair with the same talented, massaging fingers. Then sat me in the chair, rubbed a bunch of gunk in my hair, and gave me a blowjob. A blow-dry job. Not the stuff of my dreams.

She stood back and scrutinized her work. Glanced at her phone again at the picture she was working from. Like an artist painting a picture from a photo. And back at me and smiled. "Getting there!" She picked up the dreaded scissors.

Shit. In business, no one messed with me. But her. Somehow she'd one-upped me and seduced me into losing my prize beard. I stared at her, willing her to stop. Putting on my angel eyes, my hurting eyes. The eyes I used on her in college to take pity on the nerd.

She shook her head and snapped the scissors. "Don't give me those puppy-dog eyes. A deal is a deal." Her grin was pure evil. But she was as beautiful evil as she was angelic. "Hold still."

She moved in and I swallowed hard. As much from her nearness as from how close those scissors were to my jugular. If she'd wanted to slit my neck for my billions, I was completely vulnerable. Had been with her all along. She snipped away, humming to her music, smiling. Her enthusiasm for the job was almost contagious. If she hadn't been shearing me like a sheep...

And then she stepped back and studied her work again. She reached for the electric razor and turned it on with that evil glint in her eyes. "Look up and stretch out your neck. And don't move."

I grabbed her wrist. "Or what?"

"I won't be responsible if you move and I slip." She laughed again like she enjoyed teasing me.

I cursed beneath my breath and obeyed. Why hadn't I accidentally married a woman who didn't want to change me? Or did all women want to change their guys?

She buzzed and buzzed and then reached for the regular razor and the shaving cream. I'd expected her to shave the whole beard before going for the closer shave of the hand razor. But she'd just done my neck. Then again, what did a girl know about shaving a face?

She hummed and shaved. While I resisted reaching for her and pulling her into my lap. I imagined what a real marriage would be like. Pulling her into my lap. Kissing her. Taking her to the bedroom...

When she was finished with my neck, I waited for her to reach for the electric razor again. Instead, she grabbed a bottle of something from the table and poured a handful of oil that perfumed the room.

"Mmmmm! Whoever invented this scent knows women. It's almost irresistible." She rubbed it between her palms. "Beard oil. Who knew it could be so good?" She grinned at me.

Damn, I loved her right then. Loved her with all the fierceness in me. Loved her sensitive, sunny spirit. "You're done? I get to keep the beard?"

"Don't sound so incredulous! What did you think? I promised to just trim it. For now. So don't get cocky, kid. This beard's day of reckoning is coming.

"But after fighting off mobs or reporters and your assistant, there's no way I'm going to violate a clause of our agreement and lose out on all that money. I had too much fun with your credit card. So the bush stays." She winked.

"Funny, Kay." But my heart beat hard for her. She was killing me with kindness. Before my billions, few people had been nice to me. Now I had too damn many sycophants and people who played up to me because of my money. I was a sucker for real affection, but skeptical of almost everyone's motives.

She pulled a chair directly opposite me and began stroking my beard, working the oil in as she looked me in the eye. "This is the biggest night of your life, Jus. I want you to be *you* for it."

Right then, I knew I hadn't made a mistake. I grabbed her wrist. "I think I love you."

Her eyes went wide. "Tell me when you know for sure!" She cupped my chin and stared into my eyes, deflecting.

Shit, I thought. Eric had really done a number on her.

"I think I love you a little, too. Now that you've let me play with your black card. I've never bought beard oil before. You're my first."

Damn, she had me going.

"Seriously." Her face became a mask. "There's a strong chin in here. You don't have to hide behind this beard."

She knew me too well.

She leaned her forehead against mine and stroked my beard. "So soft, Jus. So touchable. I'm a wonder." She kissed the tip of my nose like I was a little boy she was humoring, and backed off.

Leaving me to swallow hard and watch her. I just needed a glimmer. A sliver of hope that she *could* love me.

She wiped her hands on a towel and grabbed a hand mirror. She spun it around and held it out to me. "I never thought I'd say this. But you are one hot, bearded guy."

She was teasing me again. She had to be. But when our eyes met, there was no hint of mocking. *Maybe it's not impossible*, I thought.

Kayla

I dressed in the guestroom and did my hair and makeup in the guest bath. He was waiting for me in the living room, like a date. Still almost a stranger to me. My heart thumped. Could I really fake it and fool his friends at the billionaires' club?

I checked my reflection in the mirror. The dresses Allie had sent over were each perfect in their way. I went with the original pink one I'd asked her for, only because the image of me wearing it was stuck in my head. Along with the thought of a pink wedding dress. When Justin had said I'd worn a pink dress to our wedding, this was the one I'd thought of. So maybe my subconscious was trying to give us a real memory. One we could take with us when this year was over. This was our big night. Justin's big night. Justin's big life. I was just along for the ride.

I tugged down the formfitting dress and touched up my lip gloss. I hadn't teased Justin. He *was* nice look-ing. Just not in a classically handsome way. But he'd grown into his face and body since college and was no longer gawky and boyish. His features were interest-ing, making him arresting to look at. And there was something attractive about a guy who didn't know he was attractive.

I hoped I'd guessed right about the style of suit I'd picked out for him.

I slid on my thousand-dollar heels, grabbed my bag and jacket, and met Justin in the living room. He was standing at the windows, looking out over the city with his back to me. The beard was hidden. All I saw was the smooth, close, stylish cut of his hair on the back of his head. This time of evening the light was still strong. He was silhouetted, the impression of shadow and time standing still highlighted by his gray suit and the collar of his black shirt peeking out.

A feeling washed over me—this was a historic moment in my life. A defining one. It was like a premonition. I'd missed the wedding, but I was a married woman now. How I handled the next year would define the rest of my life. If I could lie and fake and learn and grow, what an adventure! Something to tell my future grandchildren, whoever they were with. All about my adventures being married to the billionaire. And this was the very first exploit. The night I met the club.

I wanted to hang on to this moment. Burn the vision of him standing there into my memory so that it lasted a lifetime, fresh and new. In vibrant hues, never turning sepia with age. When he turned around, the vision would surely shatter. He would just be Justin, a casual friend from college that I barely knew now. But there was something...something about him I wanted to hang on to. *Forever.*

The suit fit Jus exactly as I imagined it would. As if it was made for him. Not a bad effect for an off-the-rack suit that had been hastily run through alterations in an afternoon. I gave a silent nod to the tailor. He was good. I wanted his name for future reference.

Jus had square, broad shoulders, and a trim waist. The perfect triangle. Slender legs that looked good in skinny-leg pants.

An athletic build, I thought with a start. More like that of a runner than a football player. But still. Athletic and Justin hadn't gone hand in hand before.

I loved the visual appeal of athletic men, apparently. I even loved the cockiness of them. And their warrior spirit. The thought that a warrior would come to my rescue and carry me off with the spoils to the temptations of the bedroom. That man, the one with his back to me at the window, looked like he could be that kind of guy. If only I hadn't known he wasn't. So there he was—my billionaire for a year.

I had a vision of what he could look like in the future, if he chose. A classy, classic businessman, strong and powerful. Totally in control. He was confident when I wasn't looking.

He must have heard me come in. He turned around. His face lit up. I was right. The illusion was shattered by the happy, boyish grin behind that beard. And the sense of awe in his voice. "You look beautiful."

He sounded as if he meant it. Not as if he was saying what was expected. Rote. The way Eric used to tell me I was beautiful. Mostly when he wanted something.

I smiled, admiring my work. "So do you."

He shrugged, so slightly it was almost imperceptible. A gesture that meant he didn't believe me.

"I mean it." I joined him at the window and ran my hands over his shoulders, straightening his suit. The fabric was soft and wonderful with the feel of luxury and money beneath my fingers.

The man was hard and firm. Still. As if he was holding his breath and nervous.

"You should wear a suit all the time," I said.

He shook his head and grinned, self-conscious. "It's surprisingly comfortable."

"Good quality is. The suit makes you look powerful, too." I grinned at him. "I can't believe Allie and I did this in an afternoon. If we'd had you in the store where you could have tried options on..."

I stretched my arms up and out, palms up. "We would have made you into one of Seattle's Most Gorgeous Guys, no problem."

He laughed again. "You're an eternal optimist and full of yourself."

"Fashion geniuses usually are. And *you* don't give yourself enough credit."

He held his hand out to me as if turning aside my praise. "Shall we?"

When I took it, it was warm and squeezed mine firmly, as if reaffirming the deal. "You still haven't told me where we're going. I don't even know what kind of car you drive."

"Depends on the day," he said, pulling me toward the door. "Tonight we're taking the car service. So we can both party like animals." His eyes danced.

"Barnyard animals, I hope. Highly appropriate at an EIEIO meeting." I squeezed his hand, enjoying the warmth of it holding mine. And the way he so easily took it and tucked my thumb beneath his. Holding hands was a small thing. But it was intimate and possessive. And I liked it. I realized with a start that Eric had stopped holding my hand a long time ago. That I'd been the one continually reaching for him. It was nice to have a guy reach for me for a change.

"We prefer Jet City Billionaires." He laughed. "Let's go."

We paused at the door of the building. The driver was waiting for us on the street, standing by the car

door, ready to throw it open for us. The throng of reporters had grown. My tweets and posts and status up-
dates had had the desired effect. The crowd of eager
journalists was waiting for a picture to go with the story of the day—Seattle's most eligible billionaire had
taken a bride. Sorry, single girls. The media had
missed the wedding. But we could give them this, the
follow up. The first night out. This was a story much
like when Bill Gates had married decades ago.

"It's almost as if someone tipped them off that we
would be making an appearance," I joked as I squeezed
his hand. "This is where we sell it. Give them what they
want—the romance of the decade. Starry-eyed newlyweds. Young, improbable love. Beautiful clothes. Im-
peccable grooming. This is the fantasy every girl
wants. American royalty."

"You mean marrying a nerd is every girl's fantasy?"
His eyes absolutely sparkled with teasing. "If only I'd
known earlier. Like junior high, when I was getting the
crap beat out of me and having my head held in the toi-
let on a daily basis. Now I see. Those big, muscly guys
were just jealous of my sex appeal. Is that what you're
saying?"

I laughed. "Those days are long gone. Junior high
girls always want the wrong kind of guys. You need to
adjust your thinking. You're rich. And you definitely
don't *look* like a nerd anymore." I took a deep breath
and thought of the crowd waiting for us to make an
appearance. "You've had media training, right?" I
should have asked earlier.

He nodded. "Yeah."

I let my breath out. "Excellent. Use it. Remember, everything is a sound bite. Don't give them anything they can clip and use out of context to make you look bad." I took another deep breath. "Now smile for the camera and follow my lead."

Justin opened the door and we were on stage. The local news crews had been joined by the entertainment rags and their fashionably dressed reporters. How had they gotten here so fast?

I felt like a modern-day princess. Much like I thought Kate Middleton probably felt her first day in the public eye as a real princess.

I wasn't a complete social bumbler. I was raised in an upper-middle-class family. That the paparazzi had absolutely zero interest in. And there's the rub. My family had a certain amount of style and good taste. But this was a new, overwhelming animal. As the cameras started flashing, I did my best to bring up some inner social diva.

There was a collective gasp as the news crews got their first look at the new, improved Justin.

"Justin! Justin, love the new look!"

"You mean the girl on my arm." He looked at me with love, faked love, but very convincingly faked, shining in his eyes. "She's gorgeous, isn't she?"

I could get used to being adored.

As the cameras clicked, I cuddled into Justin and beamed up at him as if I was doting, smitten, and so in love with him I had eyes for no one else. But I was dying, of course, to be on the entertainment news. I mean, if you were at all related to the fashion industry, this was the ultimate.

"Where did you meet?"

"How long have you been in love?"

"How did you stage a secret romance and wedding?"

"Where are you off to?"

"What about a honeymoon?"

"All the single girls across the country will be heartbroken now! Look at him, folks, the newlywed Justin Green positively glows. Who's your stylist, Justin?"

Okay, now *that* was the ultimate compliment to me.

Jus paused in the middle of the group like a seasoned professional used to being in the spotlight. "We were college sweethearts." He looked at me and smiled, though in truth the smile, which reached ear to ear, hadn't faded since we'd opened the door. "I've loved this beautiful creature since I first laid eyes on her."

That should really get Eric, the thought that Jus and I had been college lovers. I just hoped the press didn't find out about Eric and interview him. Particularly about how recently we'd broken up.

I reached up and touched Jus' cheek. Without coaching, he leaned over, pulled me into his arms, and kissed me in front of the crowd. Genius. It was the photo op they'd been looking for.

When he pulled away, we smiled into each other's eyes for a second, long enough to give them what they wanted.

"Kayla, how did you catch this guy? Let the ladies know—how do you marry a billionaire?"

"You hook them when they're young. Before they've made their billions." I laughed and squeezed Jus' arm.

"Let's see the ring? We want to see the ring."

My heart nearly stopped. And then I thought, *Why not?*

I flashed them Jus' Order of the Engineer ring and had to fight not to lose my composure and laugh hysterically when their faces fell at the sight of it. "It's Jus' prize Order of the Engineer ring. We got married on the spur of the moment and had to improvise. We're going ring shopping tomorrow for the real thing. In the meantime, this means so much to me. He's never without it." I blinked back fake tears.

He leaned in and whispered, "I thought you didn't want a ring."

"It's not for me. It's for them. And so you don't look like a cheapskate, like you said. They'll blame you for being cheap. Not me. I'm just saving your reputation."

"Thanks for that." He wasn't being sarcastic.

"Who's the lucky jeweler? What kind of ring do you have in mind?"

"Later. We'll fill you in on all the details *later*," Jus said, pulling me close. "But now, we have to go. We have a private engagement we can't be late for."

"This is the new, surprising Justin Green," one of the entertainment reporters said into her mic. "Quite a change from the private, media-shy Justin of just a few days ago. Is Kayla to credit for this change? Or is it love?"

The crowd of reporters parted respectfully for Jus and let us through, snapping pictures as Justin handed me into the car while the driver held the door for us. When we were all shut in, I leaned back against the leather seat and sighed happily.

"Jus, can you believe this? I'm wearing a dress that cost more than a month's rent. Riding in a car with a billionaire, who's my husband. We're going to be on the entertainment shows! Is this crazy or what? When we were in college, who would have predicted this? Or even imagined it? It feels like a dream. Just this morning I was worried about how I was going to pay my rent." I paused and shook my head. "This morning. It seems like a lifetime ago." I turned to look at him. "How do you live like this?"

He shrugged. "You get used to it."

"You can tell me now—where are we going?"

He grinned. "Boeing Field to catch a helicopter. That's all I know. The rest is top secret."

"Is that usual?" I said.

"For the Jet City Billionaires, it's standard operating procedure. Especially when Lazer plans the gig."

CHAPTER THREE

Kayla

"Lazer? You mean Lazer Grayson? The boy billion-aire?" I asked, impressed to the roots of my hair.

"Oh, you know him, huh? Of course you do." Justin grabbed a bottle of wine chilling in an ice bucket and popped the cork.

"I don't *know* know him. Every single girl in Seattle knows *of* him. He was voted Seattle's Best Man two years running. He's rich *and* eligible."

"And, judging from your tone, hot." Jus sighed, apparently unimpressed. "And one of my best billionaire friends. Previously the youngest member of the Jet City Billionaires." He poured two glasses of white wine and handed one to me. "To us and wedded bliss!"

"One year of it, at least!" I added, and stopped my-self from saying more. Remembering, belatedly, that even though we were alone in the car, we weren't alone in the car. The charade had to be maintained every mi-nute that we were out of the house. Every minute that we were in the house and not alone. Basically, *every* minute. "And to totally beguiling the press with our beautiful love story."

I took a sip from my crystal wineglass. It was the most heavenly wine I'd ever tasted. And my college buddy, and former sorority houseboy, Seth, had intro-duced me to some pretty fine ones. His dad owned an award-winning winery east of the mountains. "You even had *me* convinced you're madly in love with me."

"Aren't I?" he said, mildly, his eyes gesturing to-ward the driver.

"Of course you are. Just like I love you, sweetie." I leaned forward and brushed his lips with a kiss, catch-ing a whiff of that heavenly smelling beard. "After the media reaction, can you blame me for being insecure?"

"Never doubt my love for you, Kay. Never."

Traffic was surprisingly light. The drive to the air-field took no time at all. The driver took us to a private part of the airport, where a helicopter waited for us. Jus grabbed my hand and we made a run for the copter, the wind from its blades blowing my hair in my face while we ran. The pilot helped me inside.

"Jus, good to see you," the pilot said to Justin, as if they were old friends.

"You, too, Gary." Justin looked around the copter. "Just the two of us tonight?"

Gary nodded. "The rest have gone ahead. Mr. Grayson's orders. He thought you might get tied up with the press." He looked at me and back at Jus. "Congratulations, by the way."

Justin beamed. "Thanks, man. This is Kayla, my gorgeous bride.

"Mrs. Green, pleased to meet you."

I took Gary's hand and clasped it between mine. Mrs. Green! That sounded so crazy. And old. "Please, call me Kayla." I glanced at Jus and smiled. "I haven't gotten used to being Mrs. Yet. It sounds like his mom to me."

Gary laughed. "You'll get used to it soon enough."

There's no point getting used to it, I thought. *This time next year I'll be Kayla Lucas, millionaire divorcee. Free, free, free!*

Jus and I buckled in.

"Ready?" Gary asked.

Jus nodded and we were off, almost literally into the sunset. It was June, so the days were long. So not quite sunset. But getting there. The sun cast long shadows over Puget Sound and the mountains. Lighting Mt. Rainier off to the south in brilliant pink. A strawberry ice cream cone. That was what my dad called it on evenings like this.

We took off and headed west and south, over the sound into that sun. *Ocean beaches?* I wondered. Was that where we were headed?

Gary banked north. He acted as if we were out for an evening drive, in a helicopter. Just out to admire the scenery.

We rode in silence. It seemed too dangerous to say anything. At least, I was afraid I would slip. And the view from up in the blue took my breath away and made me speechless.

Beside me, Justin held my hand and smiled. It was clear we were both trying to guess where we were going. It could have been anywhere. The peninsula, Whidbey Island, the San Juans, the mountains...

As we turned more and more directly east, it became evident we were heading into the Cascades. Deeper and deeper into wooded, mountainous territory. Higher and higher. I was flying inside, too.

For an instant, I wondered why I had even hesitated about marrying a billionaire. This was the life.

It was almost a pun, but the ride flew by. Gary piloted the copter deep into the woods, high up into the mountains. To a place in the wilds where the roads ended. Over the rugged terrain until a cleared patch on the side of the mountain came into view. And a retro hunting-style lodge from the 1940s era. In the back, a deck cantilevered out over the mountain. A deck filled with people casually mingling and a glass-bottom pool that glistened like a light blue diamond.

I spotted a helipad ahead. The trees blew and bent as if bowing before royalty as we landed. Gary gently brought us down in front of the largest, most beautiful mountain lodge I had ever seen. I was experiencing a lot of firsts today. And all of them seemed larger than life. Like something out of a fairy tale.

"Lazer's lodge." Jus shook his head as if he were amused. "I should have known."

A tall, dark-haired man waited for us in the front of the house. After the helicopter landed, the man jogged toward us with athletic grace. He was young, no more than thirty. Gary jumped out and Jus handed me down to the newcomer.

As he took my hand, our eyes met. His were deep brown and sincere. Beautifully shaped, just like his full mouth and generous lips. His jaw was square. He was delightfully clean-shaved. His face so baby smooth I had to resist the urge to stroke it. He must have owned the world's best razor. Crap, I was a sucker for a smooth face.

He looked as if he should have been on a billboard in the window of a men's store, clad in only his briefs so the ladies could drool over him. I knew exactly which briefs I would put him in. And which ones I could easily imagine taking him out of.

He was immaculately dressed in a tailored suit I would bet my soul was custom made for him. Nothing short of custom would fit like that. A man who could dress himself. Be still my heart. I was ready to swoon.

It was probably unseemly, almost cheating, for a bride on what was really her wedding night, for all intents and purposes, to be inwardly drooling over another man. But ours was a marriage of convenience. We weren't in love. I was nothing more than a decoy bride. And when staring into the eyes of Lazer Grayson, what *was* a girl to do? Especially considering the spark between us.

I was a major fan girl of his. He'd been a designer on my all-time favorite game before selling it and forming a gaming networking company that I didn't understand the technical details of. Just that it had been a major innovation. He'd sold that and was now mostly an investor in other companies. He'd given me many happy hours of bashing bad guys and blowing things up. Playing kickass and beating the crap out of the guys. Lazer Grayson not only designed my favorite game, he owned major stock in all the companies that had designed my other all-time favorite video games.

Being near him brought out my inner geek girl, my inner warrior, and my not-so-inner princess. I realized with a start that one of the main male characters, my main crush in my favorite game, was clearly patterned off Grayson. Being handed out of a helicopter to him was like being handed out of a dreamy cartoon into heady real life. Right into the arms of my waiting prince.

I silently cursed my cousin Dex for getting me hooked on that damn game to begin with. And always beating me. Being this close to the game's creator made me wonder if I could get some top-secret tips out of him. Beating Dex at his own game would make my summer. And so would spending time with this man.

Lazer pulled me away from the whirr of the copter, with Jus following behind. The three of us paused at the edge of the circular drive in front of the lodge and watched the copter pull away. He smiled into my eyes. "Damn, Jus, where have you been hiding this gorgeous woman?"

His voice was as smooth and sweet as fondant on a cake. He was obviously a shameless flatterer. And I thought, *Where have you been all my life? Why didn't I meet you four days ago?*

Oh. Yeah. I wouldn't have met him *now* if not for Jus.

Jus removed my hand from Lazer's, where it had lingered too long, and put his arm possessively around my waist. "Lazer, meet my wife, Kayla. Kayla, Lazer Grayson."

I stopped myself just in time from saying, *I know who he is. Man, do I know.*

"Wife! That's just so bizarre." Lazer held my gaze, seemingly as mesmerized by me as I was by him.

Which made no sense. I was just an ordinary girl. And he was Lazer Grayson, the boy billionaire.

Justin cleared his throat.

Lazer snapped out of the trance. He slapped Jus on the back. "You tight-lipped bastard. You snowed everyone. None of us knew you even had a girlfriend." His smile sent my heart racing as he turned to me. "What do you see in this guy?"

"Jus has always been completely adorable." I leaned into my husband for emphasis. My words sounded innocuous and playful enough. But in truth, I flashed Lazer a flirty smile.

Lazer shook his head, like he didn't see the adorable in Jus. "Must be the new haircut and suit." He focused his attention on Justin. "Jus, did you finally break down and hire a stylist? God knows Ophie couldn't pick out something that nice."

"I have a wife now to do my styling. A wife with incredibly good taste. Which is why she married me." Justin sounded put out. And jealous.

Fair enough. Jealousy didn't have to mean anything other than pride was at stake. I knew the feeling, and told myself to behave and tone it down.

Lazer looked at me. "You're responsible for this?"

I smiled and nodded.

"Genius. Jus, you married a fashion genius. I can't believe you got him to get rid of that baggy sports coat and T-shirt shit he usually wears."

"Who says they're actually gone?" I said with a laugh.

Lazer arched an eyebrow comically, indicating, at least to me, that Jus was already henpecked. That I had completely pecked him into that new haircut. And how could I argue? But it was for his own good. And my pride.

Jus squeezed me tighter.

Suddenly Lazer laughed. "We'd better head in. Everyone's waiting." Lazer waved us toward the house. "Welcome to Lazer Lodge."

Lazer Lodge was the size of a respectable resort lodge. At first glance, I estimated it had to be fifteen to twenty thousand square feet. It was fashioned like a hunting lodge of the 1930s or 1940s, out of logs and river rock, with a contemporary twist. And built from the finest materials.

Lazer ushered us in.

I held back a gasp. People actually lived in this kind of magnificence?

We stepped into a large, open great room with windows along the back so large and clear it looked as if it was open air. Almost a tree house nestled in the evergreens. A row of sliding doors opened to the patio, making the place truly feel like a nest.

There was a Washington State Lottery commercial on TV where a guy lives on top of a mountain and parasails down into town for a coffee. Then zip-lines back up. I wondered whether they'd patterned it as a modest version of Lazer's Lodge. Or if Lazer had been the one to take that fantasy one step farther.

He had a breathtaking mountaintop view of the rest of the Cascade Mountains beyond. The ceilings had to be twelve feet tall at least. And something smelled delicious. A buffet was being set up on the patio.

A small crowd of fifteen to twenty people milled around on the patio.

"Come meet the members, Kayla." Lazer led the way to the patio.

The moment I stepped out, the introductions, congratulations, and ribbing flowed nonstop as Jus and Lazer introduced me to their crowd. I felt like I was drifting through a receiving line at a wedding, meeting only the groom's side. It was a blur of faces and names that danced in the air. The introductions flew too fast for me to keep track of people. Or would have, if most of the people hadn't been widely known public figures and frequently featured in magazines like *Forbes*. The terrace pulsed with the sense of power, influence, and money colliding.

Meet billionaire so and so. He made it big in the cellular technology field.

Oh, and this guy, software.

Another one, a forest industry magnate.

The congratulations to Jus on his recent IPO flowed as easily as the cocktails the waiters were passing around. *Welcome to the club* was as ubiquitous as a fight song during homecoming.

And finally, the winks, the sly looks, the congrats and backslapping over his marriage. This was a boys' club. Only one woman, the Canadian, was a billionaire in her own right. I looked around for more wives and girlfriends. They were suspiciously missing.

"There aren't many women here. Where are all the rest of the wives and girlfriends?" I whispered to Jus.

Lazer heard me and answered for him, "Girlfriends aren't allowed. Spouses rarely choose to come."

I better absorb everything, then, I thought.

I was under the microscope's eye. Sideways glances took my measure. Was I worthy of being the wife of one of their gang? Trophy-like enough? I certainly wasn't successful enough on my own to be anywhere near making this club. What other reason was there for Justin to choose me? Or was I a blatant gold digger? A mistake? Would this last the month?

Funny how I could go from feeling like I'd been raised in a respectable, middle-class family to feeling like trailer trash in an instant. Not that any of them made any accusations. They were all perfectly pleasant. So maybe it was only my insecurities sitting on my shoulder and whispering.

Beside me, Jus beamed with pride and soaked in the compliments and congrats. The men were naturally curious about my sudden appearance in Justin's life. He deflected the subtle inquiries and digs with good humor. I felt almost guilty, suddenly, for intruding on Jus' big night. For our surprise "marriage" shadowing, though not necessarily overshadowing, this night of supreme accomplishment for him.

I was awestruck by the attendees. How had he come to act so naturally and seemingly feel at home among this crowd? Little, shy Justin who everyone picked on. Seattle was home to some of the world's richest people, to the world's richest man. Many of whom were guests. Jus acted as if they were common, everyday officemates and colleagues.

Lazer was fielding questions about some work he'd had done on the lodge.

"Thank you. I've had some work done on it since last time you were here," I overheard Lazer telling the Canadian billionaire when she complimented him on it. "This is just my weekend retreat. I don't get out here as often as I should. This last winter I was here fewer than a half-dozen times. The snowmobiling and snowboarding were terrible. Not enough of the white stuff."

After ten or fifteen minutes of small talk, Lazer made an announcement. "It's time for the official induction." He herded us inside into a media room with another distracting view of the mountains and the sun that was threatening a showy sunset. He escorted Justin and me to a pair of seats in the front of the room and took the podium upfront.

"I would like to welcome all of you here tonight as we induct our newest member, our youngest member ever. The little bastard has taken the title from me. Overachiever!"

The audience laughed. Beside me, Jus smiled good-naturedly.

"I was dubbed the boy billionaire. I'd like to suggest we call the new guy the baby billionaire. If our members get any younger, they'll be in diapers."

I turned to Jus as he grabbed my hand.

"Don't worry. It's supposed to be a roast," he whispered. "It's tradition."

Lazer went on to enumerate Jus' many impressive accomplishments. Most of which I knew nothing about. A lot of the technical talk about Jus' contributions to the world of programming and software development went over my head.

"In all seriousness, he's a protégé of mine and I'm damned proud of him. Otherwise I wouldn't have nominated him for membership," Lazer said. "Ladies and gentlemen, welcome our newest member, Justin Green."

The room erupted in applause.

"And welcome our esteemed president to the platform to present Jus his key to the club."

I plastered a proud, beaming wife smile on my face, all too aware of Lazer as he left the podium and took the chair next to me. I took my phone out and looked to Lazer for confirmation that it was okay to record and snap pictures. When he nodded, I pointed my phone at Jus and smiled reassuringly.

The ceremony was quick and perfectly timed to end as the sun set over the mountains in the most brilliant hues of pink and orange, just as it had been threatening to do all evening. I caught it all on my phone.

Lazer leaned into me and whispered, "Just don't post it anywhere." His smile was sweet, but dead serious. "We value our privacy. And it won't last long anyway if you do. Our security team will hunt it down and delete it."

Wow. Just wow.

The club gave Jus a certificate and a trophy, which looked like it was made of gold, like an Oscar. He gave a short acceptance speech, thanking his family, friends, and business partners. Lazer Grayson. And the club for inviting him in. Speaking to the crowd, he was confident and funny. He threw around a few stats about the odds of becoming a billionaire that made the crowd laugh. It was almost as if he was giving a TED Talk about billionaires.

I swelled with pride, proud he was my friend. Happy I'd made the decision to help him out. He truly had a brilliant career in front of him. Dex had been right— Jus was destined for greatness. No horrible identity thief should be able to derail his life and achievements.

As the ceremony ended, a waiter appeared and served everyone a glass of champagne.

When each person had a glass, Lazer made a toast. "As you all may have heard on the news, this is an auspicious time in our baby billionaire's life. The average age for an American man to marry is now twenty-seven. Our Justin jumped the gun and tied the knot at twenty-one. He likes to do everything young—youngest billionaire ever in the club. And now a young bridegroom.

"Now I'd like to raise our glasses, not just to Justin and his impressive accomplishment, but to the newly-wed couple. Kayla, we still can't understand what you saw in him, but we wish you both happiness and joy and a long life together." He raised his glass and cheers went up. People clinked glasses with the people next to them.

"And now, business taken care of, let's do what we do best—eat and party!"

Servants appeared and opened the patio doors from the lodge to the terrace. Outside, the stars were beginning to twinkle. There was very little light pollution to interfere with them. When I looked up, the heavens seemed dizzying with their vastness and number of stars.

"Newlyweds and new inductees first." Lazer led us to the front of the line where servers waited with an assortment of food that made my mouth water, prepared by one of Seattle's finest chefs.

Lazer followed us through the line. The three of us settled at a table on the patio overlooking the pool, which was now lit only by starlight from above. It was a black pool, a dark, dizzying reflected sky filled with more stars than I remembered seeing since a childhood camping trip. A string quartet played softly at the edge of the terrace.

Lazer and Jus joked and ribbed each other like old friends, competitive friends, while I sat quietly listening and studying them both. Thinking traitorous thoughts about how hot Lazer was. And funny. And charming. And how Jus was...sweet.

The conversation turned to movies and pop culture.

"What do you think, Kay?" Jus said, putting me on the spot. "Does Lazer remind you of anyone?"

His tone was teasing and light, but there was an edge to it, too. It was as if he'd read my cheating mind and seen me watching Lazer too closely. I thanked my good luck that the lighting was dim and mostly filtered from candles and the light streaming out the doors and windows from the lodge. It hid my guilty expression.

I played along and studied Lazer openly, enjoying the chance to memorize his face. "James Bond?"

Jus laughed and grabbed another cocktail from a tray a waiter brought around. The booze flowed like water. Everyone was drinking heavily. It was Jus' fourth one. But who was counting?

"Fictional character. Close." The edge grew sharper in Jus' voice, masked by a twinkle of a joke. "He thinks Christian Grey was based on him."

Lazer laughed. "Jealous? Can I help it if women from across the country write me and ask if I was the inspiration? I've had girls show up at the gates of my house begging to meet me. Girls who've flown in, just to get a glimpse of me, Seattle's real-life young billionaire."

"Yeah," Jus said. "He's as popular as Forks since *Twilight.* You should put up a booth and make an appearance at the gates once in a while to charge them for autographs."

Lazer turned to me. "See what I have to put up with?"

I didn't reply. I was too busy trying not to laugh.

"Can I help it if women make the connection? Grey and Grayson. Same age. Both Seattle's Best Man. Youngest billionaires in Seattle's history."

"Until now," Justin said.

"We're both suave and handsome." Lazer laughed again.

"And humble," Justin said.

I laughed with them. "And the red room of pain? Is that based on you, too?"

"That's where the comparison ends." His grin was infectious and seductive.

And I thought, *Maybe he isn't into that, but I bet he's a good lover.*

Lazer winked. "I have the red room of game."

I took another sip of my cocktail, letting the alcohol take the edge off my nerves as the boys tried to one-up each other.

"Gaming nerd," Jus said, playfully. "That doesn't count. You put that in after."

"Do you have the red room here?" I asked. "Or is at another one of your homes?"

Justin stared at me in surprise, as in why would I be interested in a gaming room?

"I have a mini one here," Lazer said. "I'll show it to you later if you'd like to see it."

Jus shook his head. "Keep my wife the hell out of your red room of game, Grayson. She doesn't like video games."

Lazer laughed and gave me a conspiratorial look, mouthing, *Later.*

As the drinks continued to flow, the noise level increased. As dessert approached, Lazer seemed excited about something, as if he was keeping a secret or had planned a surprise.

"Look at this group of power players," I said to Jus and Lazer. "It's a wonder no one's come up with a conspiracy theory about you guys and your secret Jet City Billionaires."

"You mean like we plan to control the world markets and take over the world? We choose the next world leaders over poker and a cigar? We're busily planning the one-world government?" Jus put his arm around me. "Don't we?"

Lazer laughed. "Oh, definitely. You should see our war room."

I shivered. The day had been warm and pleasant, but as the dew and night fell, the patio was cool despite the strategically placed heaters.

"We're not the Bohemian Grove, Kay." Jus pulled off his suit coat and wrapped it around my shoulders.

Attentive and considerate.

"Aren't we?" Lazer made a gesture that encompassed the surroundings. "We have enough booze to qualify. My mentor has been to the Grove several times. He says it's all a bunch of guys sitting around drinking. No women allowed."

"Except for the strippers, I imagine," Jus said.

Lazer kept glancing toward the door. A waiter finally came up and whispered in his ear.

Lazer looked around the room and nodded. "I think we're ready. Bring it out."

The waiter gestured to someone inside the lodge. The string quartet began playing Pachelbel's "Canon in D." Two women dressed in white bakers' uniforms wheeled a cart out with a three-tiered wedding cake.

I gasped. I knew I was saying, or rather, thinking, every other minute since we left the city, that this or that was the most beautiful, most gorgeous thing I'd ever seen. You would think it would be getting tiresome and I would have reached my limit. But that cake really was the most beautiful one I'd ever seen. And it was from the most prestigious bakery in the city. I knew brides who'd tried to book a year, even two, ahead and couldn't get a cake. To get one on the spur of the moment in an afternoon? That was power.

Was I impressed? It sounds stupid, but this may have been the most impressive thing of the evening.

My eyes went wide. "How?"

Lazer just smiled and rose. "Go cut your cake."

Jus took me by the elbow. "Is a girl going to jump out of that thing?"

"You already have the girl." Lazer looked at me with regret.

I moved toward the cake as if in a dream, trembling as one of the bakers handed me a cake-cutting knife.

The crowd clapped as Jus cupped his hand around mine. "Ready?"

"As ever."

We cut the cake while Lazer snapped our picture on his phone. "One for the gossip rags."

I slid the slice onto a plate, picked up a fork, and filled it with cake. I held it to Jus' mouth and fed him a bite. Then he fed me one. Just like at a wedding reception. We handed the cake cutter and duties over to the bakers. I took a minute then to study the cake, with its intricate gum paste flowers and scrollwork. It was only then that I got a good look at the cake topper. And the illusion shattered. My mouth fell open. I blushed to my toes and flushed with anger.

Jus saw my distress. His gaze followed mine. "Shit," he muttered beneath his breath. He pulled the cake topper off the top tier and shook it at Lazer. "What the hell is this?"

CHAPTER FOUR

Kayla

"Who's this barefaced dude on my cake?" Jus hammed it up. Played along. He held the plastic cake topper, looking as if he might take a swing at the plastic groom. "And why is my bride all over him?" He comically cocked an eyebrow.

Lazer was laughing so hard he had to wipe a tear away. "How the hell you finally found a girl who finds you attractive is a mystery to the rest of us."

The cake topper was a clean-shaved groom holding a blond bride in his arms. Her legs wrapped around his waist and hips, climbing up him as if she couldn't wait to get him in the bedroom. She was clearly throwing herself at him. The implication was clear to me—I'd thrown myself at Jus for his money. Maybe I was being too sensitive.

Lazer looked at me as understanding dawned. "Oh, shit. Kayla, I'm sorry. I didn't think. I was just giving Justin a bad time."

The string quartet continued playing in the background. But the crowd of billionaires had gone largely silent, enjoying the show.

And then I realized that Lazer really *hadn't* meant to imply I was a gold digger.

Maybe it was the buzz from the alcohol. Maybe it was the completely ludicrous situation. And all the faking it. Maybe I was just tired. But suddenly, it *was* funny.

I set down the piece of cake I'd been holding, hitched up my short skirt, and threw my arms around Jus. "Pick me up," I whispered to him, and threw my legs around his waist, mimicking the pose. Then I pulled him into a passionate, bright kiss to raucous applause.

"How was that? Did that look right?" I said to the crowd. "Look at this guy and tell me he isn't hot!"

The software mogul flashed me the okay sign as I started laughing.

Someone called out, "Looks like you got the right girl, Green."

I think then I earned the respect of the Jet City Billionaires' Club. If you can't laugh at yourself, who can you laugh at?

Jus was beaming as he set me down and kissed me again for good measure. He looked exactly like a happy groom *should* look.

"Hey, Lazer," I said, lightheaded from the cocktails and the events of the day. I grabbed the cake topper. "You couldn't get one with a bearded groom?"

"In an afternoon? No," Lazer joked back. "Not even I have that much power and money."

I set the topper down. "Let us eat cake!" I grabbed Jus, and my plate of cake, and pulled him away from the serving table.

We mingled, hand in hand. It quickly became apparent the guys wanted to talk to Jus about business. Given Jus' business, you would think it would have been interesting talk about fashion and retail merchandising. But these techie types were more interested in his programming. Or the complicated details of running a retail business and managing a multibillion IPO. A unicorn. I quickly grew bored.

Ever the gracious host, Lazer was suddenly at my elbow. "This must be boring as hell for you. Let me show you the house."

"I'd love that!" I'd been dying to see it since we arrived. I turned to Justin. "Do you mind?"

Jus was engaged deep in conversation. He nodded. "Just keep her out of that game room."

Lazer grinned at him, took my elbow, and guided me toward the house. "I hope you didn't promise to honor *and* obey him?"

I laughed. No, I hadn't, actually. All I'd really promised was not to blow the cover of our convenient marriage. "Obey? No way."

"Good." Lazer's grin was devilish and made my heart race.

If I wasn't mistaken, there was chemistry between us. It was just too bad I was a married woman. He couldn't know I was married in name only. And life, with its merciless sense of humor, prevented me from telling him.

"Let me show you the house." He leaned in to whisper in my ear. "Game room and all. Jus is worried I'll show him with my superior gaming skills. Not many guys can last longer or penetrate deeper than I can. Into a game."

Was Lazer flirting with me? That wasn't full of innuendo and double meaning. Guys! Always bragging about their prowess.

"I suppose you never go soft on anyone," I said, flirting and playing along.

He raised an eyebrow. "Definitely not. I'm not one of those limp-thumbed players. I'm hard...on everyone."

"How long are we going to keep this up?"

"I can keep it up all night." There was that sensual tone of his. "I'm having fun."

I flashed him my flirty smile and rolled my eyes.

"Anyone ever tell you this one? Gaming is like sex. You never know how long it's going to last."

I lost it. "You *are* bad."

"This is nothing. I can be worse. What's wrong? You don't like innuendo?"

"Innuendo is not an Italian suppository, you know," I said. "And I'm a blushing new bride."

"I don't see you blushing." He sounded almost regretful as he guided me down a hallway off the great room and became suddenly serious. "I'm sorry about out there." He nodded toward the patio. "The cake."

"There's no need to apologize." I looked away from him.

"But I'd like to. I was thoughtless. I didn't think about your feelings. I didn't think about anything but teasing Jus. He's so boyishly innocent around girls. He wouldn't know what to do with a girl if she threw herself at him."

I put my hand on my hip and gave him a look that said, *Really?*

"So I was wrong!" He laughed softly. "Justin getting married out of the blue shocked everybody. He hasn't had two dates in a row since I met him. A girlfriend?" He made a sound of disbelief and rolled his eyes. "How in the hell did he find you and keep you a secret?

"Since he started Flashionista he's been working twenty-four-seven. He's barely had time for a catnap. Let alone a relationship, serious or otherwise. And then here you are—" He halted, and sighed as if frustrated with himself. "A girl who's definitely out of his league. You must be the most understanding woman on the planet."

I looked at him and arched an eyebrow.

"I'm still messing this up, aren't I?"

I laughed. "Yes, you are."

He turned to face me and pointed to the room off to our right without looking at it. He was staring me in the eye. "You've seen the media room. I use it for parties and business meetings, like tonight."

"Yes. Gorgeous room. Perfect space for it," I said without breaking his gaze.

"We affectionately call him the virgin billionaire. Damn you," he said. "We'll have to come up with something else now. There's no way it will be as wickedly funny."

He had my full attention. *Was* Jus really a virgin?

"I tried one or twice to set him up. He joked he didn't have time to be distracted by a woman." Lazer shook his head, as if he still couldn't believe Jus had married me. "I had no idea he was seeing someone. *You.* That's what made the cake topper so damn funny. The only way Justin was going to get a girl was if she stripped naked and threw herself at him."

I fought to keep my composure and not laugh at the absurdity of things. "I see. You think I threw myself at him? For his money?"

"I don't think anything—"

"You're an empty-headed billionaire?" I raised an eyebrow. "How disappointing. I like men with substance."

His eyes lit up. "You don't back down."

"You don't like being challenged," I shot back.

When he grinned, he was devastating in his perfection. "I take pride in knowing what's going on. With businesses I'm invested in and my friends."

"Am I a threat to either?" I felt bold.

"Time will tell."

I couldn't help noticing little things about him. Like how good he smelled. How white and straight his teeth were. How strong his chin was. How thick the dark stubble on it was. How the electricity crackled between us.

I shrugged. "For your information, we had a whirlwind four-hour romance. Our engagement was even shorter. I think you could measure it in minutes. We knew each other in college. Bumped into each other in Reno. Hours later, we were married. Does that allay your fears?"

Marry in haste. Wait a year. Collect ten mil. Repent with an even hotter billionaire at leisure. Great new plan?

Lazer was staring at me with an appraising look in his eye. "So you *did* throw yourself at him?"

The identity thief had. If I was supposed to be her, then yes.

I shrugged. "Maybe."

Lazer took my elbow and started walking again. "I'm going to keep my eye on you."

"Please do."

His laughter echoed off the walls. "You make it hard to apologize."

We stopped inconveniently at the doorway to a lavish bedroom, complete with a fireplace and bearskin rug that looked perfect for a round of lovemaking.

"I was a complete douche for not thinking my gag through all the way." He looked and sounded genuinely apologetic. "I'm sorry."

"That's okay. Douches have always been my kind of guy." I almost snorted. I was thinking of Eric. But Lazer couldn't know that.

His eyes lit up. He squinted as if studying me. "That's too damn bad. You've picked the wrong man. Justin is the least douchey guy I know."

"If it doesn't last, we'll know why, then, won't we?" I turned my attention to the bedroom before I gave everything away. "Very nice. Love the fireplace. And the rug." I smiled at him. "Your guests must be very comfortable here."

"Yes, I hope so. I have eight guestrooms. They're all fairly similar, done in lodge style. Each has its own bathroom suite. Let me show you."

Being alone in a bedroom with him made me feel incredibly guilty. Mostly because of the thoughts I was having about him. This afternoon when I'd signed up for this job, I would never have imagined meeting a man who piqued my interest like Lazer did so soon, if at all. Hadn't I sworn off men just a few days ago? Life was a bitch.

I murmured and cooed about how fabulous the bathroom was, and we left the bedroom. He showed me the rest of the house, talking about his vision for it and how his interior designer had implemented it. It could have sounded pretentious. But the passion in his voice was genuine.

I loved design of any kind, so I was fascinated. And fighting to keep from gaping the entire time.

Lazer and I connected on so many levels. As we talked, we discovered we had enough common interests to score high on any compatibility test. There was so much about him that was perfect. Lazer was twenty-eight, mature, and sophisticated compared to Jus and his boyish charm. I'd always liked guys who were a few years older. Being in Lazer's company felt right. I was fighting crushing on him.

We reached the end of the tour.

"I saved the best for last." He opened a door and the lights magically came on. "The red room of game!"

I peeked inside. "It's not so red, really." Though the logs of the walls had a reddish hue and there were red accents here and there. Red pillows with outdoorsy designs. Prints with red themes. "But it is magnificent." I took a step inside. "Look at all your gaming systems! And the retro games."

His eyes lit up. "From your reaction earlier, I'm guess you like video games?"

"I'm a casual gamer. I mostly play with my cousin. He generally beats me. But I'm your biggest fan girl. I played the game you developed before you moved on to networking. Loved the character of yourself you put in. Meeting you is like—" I caught myself in time. The alcohol had loosened my lips. "It's a thrill."

"Thrill, is it? I like that." His eyes danced.

"Narcissist!"

He laughed. "Would you like to play the new game my good friend is launching soon? It's not on the market yet. It's just about to go into alpha testing. You'd be one of the first people outside the company to play. Of course, you'll have to swear on your life you won't tell a soul a thing about it. Or I'll have to kill you."

I lost the battle. My mouth fell open. "Are you kidding? Do you want a blood oath? Or will a pinkie swear do?"

He laughed and led me deep into the room. "If you tell anyone you were playing, I'll deny it."

"I can keep a secret, believe me." I was getting myself deeper and deeper into secrets.

He explained the game while he set it up. His passion was catching as he talked about its development, the creativity behind it, the storytelling. "I own a decent chunk of the company."

He sat down on the plush leather sofa next to me and handed me a controller. And then we were playing. Real gamers don't play like the actors on TV, hands flying, bodies moving. Real gamers barely move their thumbs and hold their controllers steady. Gaming is a mind and thumb activity.

Lazer was subtle, and good, as he guided and coached me. Both of us laughing. Making jokes. And bragging when we did something brilliant. Which he did more often than I did. But it *was* his game. He had the inside knowledge.

I squealed and laughed like a teenage girl as we played. He was the warrior king. I was his warrior queen. Saving the world together. I was hyperaware of everything about him. The way he concentrated. The smell of his cologne. The way his arm accidentally brushed mine from time to time. Why? Why hadn't I met him earlier?

"I would love to live in this video world," I said at one point. "It's"—I stared at him—"awesome. A real fantasy." He was awesome.

He paused and turned to me. "Your wish is my command, my queen. You can live in this world forever. Say the word and I'll make you a character in it."

Okay, were my eyes as big and round as they felt? Were the joy, awe, and surprise blatant on my face? In that instant, my heart beat for him. "Immortality? Are you serious?"

His sexy grin almost made my heart stop. "If you want to live forever, I'm your guy. Send me a favorite picture of yourself. I'll get my friend's artists right on it. Top priority. With any luck, your character will make it into the alpha test version. The guys who play the game will love you." He used that sensual tone on purpose, wielding it as effectively as his character swung a sword onscreen.

He knew how to flatter a girl. But then, when it came to him, it didn't take much. What he didn't supply, me and my hopeless optimism did. I was a complete pushover around him. "Can they make me a hot warrior princess?"

"Oh, baby, they won't even have to use their imagination."

Was he flirting with me? He had to be flirting with me. I should have been cautious. Maybe he was testing to see how loyal I was to his protégé Jus. Just how easily could I be parted from my billionaire if I was flattered by another, smoother, more seductive, more mature, more attractive one? How much of a gold-digging girl was I?

I was pleasantly buzzed from one too many highly delicious, skillfully made cocktails. The drinks Lazer served were so smooth, they went down like water.

Some people were mean drunks. I was a flirtatious one. I felt positively kittenish, as if I could curl up in Lazer's lap and purr. Couldn't help myself. It used to make Eric furious when I flirted back with his fraternity brothers at drinking functions. Something about alcohol took away my inhibitions and blew past my good sense. It was harmless. *Usually.* In this case, I wasn't so sure.

"It will be a minor character," he said. "Not a main, playable one."

"Fine by me."

"Would you like to be an alpha tester and see your character in action?"

"You really are my knight in shining armor! Put me in, please!"

His smile was disarming. "I warn you. It's as much work as play. You have to play the game to catch bugs."

"Not a problem!" My fan-girl side had abandoned any pretense of playing it cool and was positively gushing.

"You're in. I'll get you set up tomorrow. You really will have to sign a nondisclosure then. And not tell anyone about the game. Or even that you're testing it."

"I can keep a secret. Believe me." I couldn't stop smiling. "I can't believe this. My cousin is going to be *so* jealous! Pea green!"

"Should I be jealous, too?"

At the sound of Jus' voice, I literally jumped. I spun around to see him standing in the doorway, looking at us as shocked as if he'd caught us sleeping together. How long had he been standing there? And how much had he heard?

Justin

"Ooooh. That felt good. Hit me again!"

At the sound of Kayla's voice, I froze in the hallway outside Lazer's damn game room.

"You like that? Good. Beg for more, baby." Lazer's voice was slick with adrenaline.

Shit. My heart hammered. I was afraid of what I would find when I looked in the room. Kay was breaking my heart.

"You're going to make me beg? You sadistic bastard." Kayla laughed. "Quick! Unchain me."

The door was open. How bad could it be? I screwed up my courage and stood in the doorway, forcing myself to look.

Kay and Lazer sat next to each other on the sofa, game controllers in hand, thumbs flying, playing Lazer's hottest investment's newest creation. Damn him! He *would* seduce her with that girly fantasy game.

They were so absorbed that neither of them heard me approach. I clenched my jaw so hard the muscle in my cheek ticked. What the hell? Kayla played like she was experienced. How had she hidden that from me?

Lazer was coaching her. Expertly. Patiently. Intimately. And sitting way the hell too close to my wife.

As they played, they laughed and joked like soul mates. Moving together and interacting with their characters. Easy in each other's company. And damn it, they looked like they were made for each other. *I* felt like the one intruding on *their* honeymoon.

The chemistry between them fairly crackled. I'd seen it the moment he'd helped her down from the copter. I'd seen that same look on her face in college when she'd looked at Eric. On screen, Lazer's studly king kneeled before her buxom queen and presented her with a prize. How chivalrous of him.

I shouldn't have let her come. I should have kept her the hell away from Lazer. Women loved him too easily. He did nothing but break their hearts.

But this was different. Look at them. Shit, *look* at them! They were the perfect couple. Lazer, tall, dark, handsome, charming, and rich. Kay so beautiful that looking at her made my heart tight.

He'd barely met her and already he'd enticed her into playing his game. I had no idea Kay was into this kind of activity. A girl like her enjoying video games? It seemed out of character.

I was her husband. *I* should have been the one to introduce her to the art of gaming. I clenched my fists at my side and willed myself to calm down. I felt betrayed and jealous as hell—she'd played with him first.

I stood in the doorway for a good minute, watching Kay and Lazer, before my jealousy got the best of me and announced myself before I was ready. "Should I be jealous, too?"

Kay jumped. They turned and looked over their shoulders at me, guilt as clear on their faces as if I'd walked in on them.

"Yeah, jealous you aren't playing with us. I was just showing Kayla the new game." Lazer always had been quick on his feet. "Come in and join us, buddy!" Lazer waved me in.

"Another time." I'd had too much to drink. It had been a hell of a day. I started the day expecting to be a single man again. Not a jealous husband. I was riding on a volatile edge. "It's getting late. Gary will be arriving with the copter any minute."

Kayla set her controller down and glanced at her watch. She flushed so deeply, it was evident even in the intimately lit room. "Sorry, Jus. I didn't realize we'd been gone so long."

She stood, slipped her shoes on, grabbed my jacket that had been thrown over the back of the sofa, came over to me, and slid her arm through mine. "Thanks for the sneak preview, Lazer. And everything tonight. I'll never forget my only EIEIO meeting."

She leaned her head against my arm as if to make amends while I wrapped my suit coat around her shoulders.

Lazer dropped his controller and stood, too. "I'm glad you came. I'll show you out."

I almost told him not to bother. But why look even more like a jealous prick? Lazer was just being Lazer.

By the time we said our goodbyes and made our way to the front door, the copter was waiting for us. I made a point of being in good humor and pushing my jealousy aside.

But as I grabbed Kayla's hand and ran with her to the copter, I made a vow. I wasn't losing her to Lazer. Not if I could help it.

CHAPTER FIVE

Kayla

We rode back in the helicopter in stony silence. With Jus' bag with his award in it between us. Although, what really is stony about silence? We sat in some kind of silence, anyway. Jus seemed upset. I was contemplative. There was so much I wanted to say. So much I wanted to explain. None of which I could do in front of Gary.

The copter took off into the dark, starry sky. To the howl of a coyote in the distance. The ride should have been romantic. If I'd been a real bride I would have curled up next to Jus and whispered how eager I was to get him home. How gorgeous the night sky was. How gorgeous he was. And how this was a night I'd never forget.

But I didn't want him thinking it was Lazer I wouldn't forget. The cold night air had sobered me. I sat with my hands demurely folded in my lap, looking out over the dark forests and thinking being dropped into the middle of them was almost preferable to being frozen out by Jus.

The car met us at the airfield. We rode home in silence in the car, too. Just this morning I'd been blissfully single. With no thought of marriage. Now I was having seconds thoughts about the contract I'd signed. Could I handle 364 more days of faking *everything everywhere*? Pretending I was in love with a guy I really barely knew now. Turning away other men. Gorgeous men. Charming men. Men I had instant chemistry with. Letting other delicious, desirable opportunities slide by. On the other hand, financially speaking, what other opportunity would pay off as handsomely as this one? Would have as many other side benefits and beautiful clothes?

Or would I screw up time after time as I had this evening? Make us into tabloid fodder? Would I crack? Jus had asked for one condition—that I not embarrass him with other guys. In his eyes, had I already violated the agreement?

I didn't know what I wanted anymore. This had all been thrust on me. I hadn't had time to think through all the consequences.

Neither of us spoke until we were safely inside the penthouse.

"I'm sorry," I blurted out the moment the door closed behind us. I couldn't hold it in any longer.

Jus set the bag he was carrying with his award in it on the sofa and gave me a questioning look.

"I've done something to upset you," I said. "Was it throwing myself at you while we were cutting the cake? Was that too much? Not funny? Or going off alone with Lazer, is that it? We just lost track of time playing the game. You've been lost in a game before. You know how that goes."

His jaw was set. He looked at me, but he didn't acknowledge me. He stood incredibly still.

I wondered if he was regretting taking me to the meeting. Wishing he'd taken adoring Ophie along instead. She wouldn't have embarrassed him by gaming with Lazer. No, she would have spent the evening appropriately fawning over Jus. Like a bride who was desperately in love with him should.

I took a deep breath and made a split-second decision. "I can leave now if you want. Call the deal off. I'll sign anything you want waiving any rights." I sighed. "I don't know if *I* can do *this*."

"You mean pretend to be in love with me?" His expression was a mask. "It's not that hard. Just pretend I'm Lazer." He snorted as if not quite amused. As if I'd hurt his feelings.

I'd probably just embarrassed him.

"In my defense, I'm a flirty drunk," I said. "You remember that from college, right?"

"You never flirted with *me*." His voice was hard.

"We never went drinking together, did we?" I didn't think we did, but I honestly couldn't remember. He'd been too young to get into the bars and he wasn't in a frat.

"No." He frowned, looking as if he was recalling unpleasant memories.

"But I told you my funny drinking stories and how Eric used to blow up at me."

He frowned.

The more I talked, the more I messed things up. I took a deep breath. "Call the car service and I'll go. We'll think of something else to save your reputation." I slid his jacket off and held it out to him.

"A deal's a deal, Kay." He sounded angry. "You can't back out because of one small slipup. On our first day. Give us time to grow into this role. We're both in too deep now. There's no going back."

I nodded. "I'm not backing out. I'm giving you an out."

"I don't want a damn out!" He took a deep breath. "I'm just...it's just...damn, I wanted to be your first." There was a tiny smile playing at the edge of his lips, as if he was trying to break the tension.

I stared at him and played along. "First? You know I've gamed before?"

"No, I didn't know you played. You never played with Dex and me in college. I thought you were inexperienced. A gaming virgin. It's something a husband should know."

"I played with Dex."

He shook his head. "Everyone played with Dex. Hell, I played with Dex."

I smiled. "You're right. I *should* have told you." I put a tease in my voice. "Before we signed that postnup. I had no idea it was a deal breaker. I'm coming clean now."

I sighed. "It's my dirty secret. I kind of have a reputation for being a secret gaming slut. With Dex, mostly. But also with Eric and his frat brothers, too. In college, I was able to keep it from my sorority sisters. And even act like it was beneath me. But the houseboys knew. Sometimes I sneaked down to game with them, too. In the basement." I took a deep breath. "Does that change the way you feel about me?"

He looked me in the eye. "I wanted to be your first...something."

"You are. You're my first husband." I gave him a shaky smile. "No one will ever take that away from you or us. You'll always be my most important first." I took a step toward him.

He held his arms out for me. I threw myself into them and rested my head against his hard, broad chest.

"I don't deserve you, my darling trophy wife." His heart was hammering wildly.

I looked up at him, past that damned beard. "Is this our first fight?"

"I think it is." He squeezed me tight. "We made it through, what? Eighteen hours of wedded bliss before we started to argue. Do you think we're doomed?"

"I know we're doomed. Our marriage has an expiration date." I laughed softly and batted my eyes at him in an exaggerated way. "Am I forgiven for gaming with another guy?"

"Stop batting your eyes at me like that!" He sighed, acting as if he was exasperated.

I batted them more enthusiastically. "Only if you forgive me."

"Stop that! You look like you have something in your eye." He smiled outright.

I made kissy lips at him.

"Uncle! I forgive you. You're obviously not the first person to do something stupid when they've had too much to drink. Given the situation we're in, I can hardly talk."

I smiled at him, more relieved than I expected to be. I'd regretted my offer almost the minute the words slipped out. I stopped the wild eyelash fluttering. What had I been thinking? I wasn't ready to leave him and face marital failure after less than twenty-four hours. How would I explain that to my family? I wasn't a quitter. And life with him *was* exciting.

"I brought you something from the party." He pried loose from me and went to the sofa to rustle through his bag.

His back was to me as I imagined all kinds of things. Like a delicious piece of our wedding cake, for example. To put in the freezer and serve with champagne when we divorced on our first anniversary. It would have been thoughtful, actually, for Lazer to send the extra cake home with us. Maybe if we hadn't left in such a hurry...

I was picturing Lazer with his shirtsleeves rolled up. The intense look on his face. The fine curve of his biceps. The way my heart fluttered around him.

Jus turned around suddenly.

I wiped my face clear of thoughts of Lazer just in time.

Jus held out that offending cake topper to me. "For you, my dear. So you can smash it to smithereens." He balanced it in the palm of his hand.

It seemed symbolic of the whole delicate, precarious nature of our faked marriage. It *had* been a long day. That was my excuse for my heart going soft and mushy. And tears standing in my eyes. Jus was the sweetest guy I knew. In that moment, he looked completely, adorably vulnerable. At least I hadn't married a douche.

When I took the statue from him, our hands brushed. I was left wondering if I imagined a tiny spark. Or was the air just particularly dry?

"This is made from resin," I said. "It's going to be hard, if not impossible, to smash. Now if it were more expensive ceramic—"

He frowned. "Damn that tightwad Lazer. I'll get you a hammer." He turned toward the kitchen. "I have one around here somewhere. It's probably in the junk drawer."

A lump formed in my throat. I grabbed his arm. "Smash the topper from our only wedding cake? Are you kidding? This is going in my keepsake box. Since I wasn't at our wedding, and you can't remember it, we have to grab what memories we can for posterity."

He looked startled, and happily, surprisingly touched. He wrapped his arms around me and hugged me. "You're right. Thanks, Kay."

I felt warm and safe in his arms. Which had to be a good sign.

"It's late," he said after the hug had lasted an indecently long time. "I have to get up early. We should go to bed."

Yes, bed. Definitely. "Oh. Right. Agreed. Guestroom?" I pointed in its general direction.

He shook his head. "Magda will be here in the morning. She arrives bright and early to make my breakfast. She insists on it. For appearances' sake, you should probably sleep with me."

"Um, yes. Of course. Is it just me, or did we not think all the details through?"

He grinned and took my hand. "Not you. We're definitely playing this on the fly." He squeezed my hand. "Don't worry. I have a king-size bed." He paused and made a funny expression. "And no one's ever told me I snore."

I laughed. "The bigger question is whether you sleep in the middle?"

"I sleep anywhere I feel like it. But you're small. You'll be fine. You don't take up much room."

"I just remembered. I left my clothes in the guestroom. Should I get them?" I set the cake topper down on the nearest end table.

"Good thinking. Yeah, probably." He pulled me toward the guestroom, where we picked up my clothes and carried them to his room.

I realized, with a start, that I hadn't gotten a tour of the complete penthouse. This was my first glimpse at his private domain. As he pulled me into the room, I felt like an interloper in his private space. Everything in the room was black, gray, silver, and red—the bedding, the furniture, the accent pieces.

We dumped my clothes on an oversize red armchair in the corner. I would argue for closet space tomorrow.

"The bathroom's there." He pointed.

I hesitated. "The thing is—I don't have a nightgown. Or a toothbrush."

"No problem. You can sleep in the nude. I won't be offended." His eyes danced.

"In your dreams!" I put my hands on my hips. "For tonight, I need a shacker shirt."

He just stared at me.

"You know, one of your T-shirts to sleep in?"

"I know what a shacker shirt is. Being the nerd I am, I've never given a girl one before."

I laughed. "Good. Now I get to be your first. How about you? Do *you* sleep in the nude?"

He grinned. "When the mood strikes or I need to do laundry."

"Sooo," I said. "What does your laundry hamper look like?"

He laughed. "Relax. I'm a man of my word. And Magda did the laundry yesterday." He went to his polished black dresser, pulled out a clean T-shirt, and tossed it to me. "You can sleep in this.

"Need anything else? A toothbrush? Toothpaste? Magda stocks the guestrooms with toiletries. Tomorrow, if we have time, we'll make a run to your apartment. Or I can send someone over to pick up a few things. We'll make arrangements to move over whatever you want."

I looked around his room and frowned. As masculine as it was, there was nothing inexpensive about it. "Even my best things will look cheap in this room."

He shrugged as if he couldn't care less. "For the next year, it's your home, too. Bring whatever you like."

I nodded, still uncertain, and wandered into the bathroom to change. And crap, which is sort of literal considering the room, one wall of the bathroom was windows floor to ceiling. With no curtains. The most beautiful black claw-foot tub stood by itself next to the windows. So he could bathe in the stars. Or shower. There was a shower with black and red tiles right next to it. He even had black towels.

I wasn't shy about my body. But I generally liked privacy in the bathroom. I huddled as far from the windows and changed as quickly as I could.

When I came out, he was standing in his boxer briefs and T-shirt, waiting with an armful of toiletries.

"Your bathroom has no curtains," I said, accusing him of something. Though I wasn't sure what, exactly.

"I know. Isn't it gorgeous?" When he saw my face, understanding dawned. He laughed. "Don't worry. No one can see you. We're above everyone else."

"You do realize how snooty that sounds?" I said.

"Just stating the facts." He brought the toiletries into the bathroom and dumped them on the counter between the two sinks. Magda had good taste. The guest supplies were all high-end brands.

"This is very domestic," I said as we brushed our teeth side by side with our backs to the windows.

He smiled at me in the mirror and winked. But I refused to floss my teeth in front of him.

When we were finished, we went back into the bedroom and hesitated, awkwardly, at the foot of the bed, staring at it as if it were the enemy.

He cleared his throat. "We can't stand here all night. One of us is going to have to make a move. Which side do you want?"

"Which side do you usually sleep on?"

"You're hedging," he said. "I asked you first. You're my guest. You pick."

"Guest?" I laughed. "I'm no guest. I'm your wife. You realize that which side we sleep on will define our entire relationship? Forever."

"You mean for a year?" he said, deadpan.

"Yeah. That. Which side do you usually sleep on?"

He shrugged. "Whichever side is most comfortable at the moment. Don't overthink it, Kay."

I threw back the covers and climbed into the right side out of habit, really. It was the side I always took with Eric. "Satisfied?"

He grinned, turned out the light, and went to his side of the bed, slipping off his shirt off before he climbed in. I got the barest glance of the planes of his back and the definition of his muscles. He was surprisingly well built.

He pulled the covers up and turned his back to me. "'Night, Kayla."

I wondered at his self-control. Maybe I'd misread the desire in his eyes earlier. Maybe he wasn't into me anymore. Then what the hell was that drunken Reno wedding all about? I flipped and I flopped—he wants me. He wants me not.

His bedroom had two full walls of windows high above the city. And no curtains on any of them. Just stars and the moon. Lying there in that room with no curtains, I was tired and wide awake at the same time. I balled my fists and silently cursed him for drifting off to sleep so quickly. *Just like a guy,* I thought. Didn't he realize what we'd done?

When I woke in the morning, our marital bed was empty. On so many levels. When I glanced at the clock, it was way too early to be out of bed. But somehow Jus was. My head pounded as I got up, wondering if he'd already left the house for the office. What was I supposed to do with my day? What did this job as his wife entail?

I heard the soft whir of appliances coming from the great room and the murmur of voices. I thought I even heard Jus' laugh. I headed out without putting on a robe. Mostly because I had no robe to put on.

I still had bedhead and my eyes were dewy with sleep. I walked into the great room to find Jus sitting at the breakfast counter, and a middle-aged woman of indeterminate ethnicity humming and moving about the kitchen. I remembered too late what Jus had said about the housekeeper coming in early to make him breakfast. I probably should have gotten dressed before coming out. Which peeved me. Was there no privacy anywhere? And now that I thought about it—what was I supposed to dress in? All I had were what I'd worn yesterday and evening clothes.

I was just about to turn around when Jus spotted me. For a moment before he masked his expression, I swore I saw desire. His eyes lit up. "Kay! There's my beautiful bride."

Crap. Let the acting begin. It was too early for convincing acting. I was a morning grump and needed my coffee before I did anything. I forced myself to smile and boldly walked over to him and looped my arms around him, trying to tantalize him with my braless breasts. Even Data was thought it was too early. She was curled up in her doggy bed.

He took the opportunity to exercise his fake marital rights and feel me up. Right in front of the help. And I couldn't even give him a dirty look. Then again, I had brought it on myself. I kissed him lightly, going for a good-morning peck. He kissed me back with passion a guy on his honeymoon should have.

"Newlyweds!" Magda mumbled, but she sounded pleased enough, though suspicious of my motives.

"You look like you need coffee," Jus said. "We have just about every coffee machine known to man here— Keurig, espresso machines, pour-over devices, and regular old coffee machines. Take your pick. Magda will make you whatever you want."

Jus pulled me around even with where he sat on a barstool at the breakfast counter and slid his arm around my waist. "Magda, meet Mrs. Green." There was a smile in his voice like it was a big joke. He knew I wasn't taking his name. And I wouldn't be Mrs. Green long, anyway.

"Kay, Magda, the best cook and housekeeper in the world!" There was that boyish enthusiasm again.

It put a smile on her face even as she scrutinized me. There was that look again, the one the billionaires and the press had given me. It wasn't constrained by social status or occupation. People, one and all, gave me what I decided to call the gold digger look. Part suspicion. Part disgust. Part "too bad she got there first, the poor boy is besotted and can't see her for what she is."

I wanted to scream and yell, *No fair! Not true! Don't make snap judgments when you don't know the facts.*

But because that would blow the whole cover, I kept my mouth shut and smiled sweetly. I would just have to show them. Then I thought, *Oh, wait. Fat chance.* I was pretty much doomed to keep that association for the rest of my life. In a year, when we divorced, I would seal my fate of gold-digging woman forever.

I hadn't thought through the damage to my reputation before I signed on the dotted line. Did it really matter what strangers thought of me and my motives? I would have to learn to live with it.

"So nice to meet you," I said with the cursed smile fixed in place as I ran my hand idly through Jus' hair like I used to do to Eric.

I had to play the adoring wifey, didn't I? Crap, I hated the term wifey.

"Nice to meet you, too, Mrs. Justin." Her accent was an odd combination of Mexican and Eastern European, and her tone was anything but happy. "What kind of coffee can I get you? We have everything. I'm a trained barista. I can make anything."

"A caramel mocha?"

She nodded and got to work.

"You weren't kidding about getting up early," I said to Jus. "When are you off to the office?"

He smelled deliciously of beard oil. Which made me ridiculously pleased that he was using it.

He glanced at his watch. "As soon as I finish my orange juice. Freshly squeezed. Like a glass?"

I shook my head. "No thanks. How busy is your day?" I glanced at my ring finger. "We have a few things to do. I told the press we were going ring shopping today."

"My baby wants jewels, is that it?" He gave me a squeeze.

"I don't want to be a liar right out of the box." Too late for that. "And I'd like to have a ring before you meet my parents on Friday."

He grabbed his phone and brought up his calendar. "I wasn't planning to take any time off today. I already burned one day—" He looked suddenly sheepish. "Anything for you, baby." There was a teasing twinkle in his eyes.

Baby, sweetie, honey, dear, hey you? We hadn't even had time to settle on our pet endearment for each other. I thought "sugar daddy" sounded pretty good for him. If I was going to play a ruthless moneygrubber for a year, why not?

As he scrolled through his day, he pursed his lips. "I can postpone my one o'clock and take a late lunch." He glanced at me. "I'll make an appointment at the engagement ring store. You can meet me there. Just remember, if you don't find a ring you like, there's no pressure to buy one today. You're going to have it a long time."

Oh, he was good. He sounded totally genuine. And maybe he was. Maybe I would have his ring a long time, locked in a jewelry box somewhere as a reminder of my year of Jus. While he was off with his seventh wife or something. Didn't billionaires go through wives like water? Or was that just a stereotype?

I nodded. "May I use the car service? I need to run by my apartment and pick up a few things." Like my birth control pills. In all the excitement, I missed yesterday's. Not like it mattered. But without it my periods were hell.

I'd heard of couples being too tired to do the deed on their wedding night. It had always sounded crazy to me. And here I was, an untouched bride for the duration. By agreement.

I smiled sweetly at him. I had another motive, too— to get away from Magda's prying eyes. I got the distinct impression she was protective of Jus and felt as if I was intruding on her territory. This was the problem with bachelors and housekeepers. They let the housekeepers run things and get overprotective of their charges. Give me a week and I would wrest control from her.

"Sure. Magda has the number and can help you with anything you need. You aren't going to work today?" He watched me.

"Nope. I'm calling in rich!" I clapped, gleefully. I couldn't wait to ditch that job.

It was the wrong thing to say in front of Magda. Her back stiffened and, although she was pleasant enough as she handed me my coffee, her eyes were hard.

"I'm going to quit," I said to soften it. "The business is in trouble. They've been cutting my hours for months. My boss will be relieved she won't have to lay me off."

"Good," Jus said. "My wife deserves a more prestigious job than...what is it you do?"

He was really going to make me talk about men's underpants in front of the help?

"Shut up! I'm a men's furnishings merch buyer and you know it." Though I actually wasn't sure he did. Had it come up in conversation?

"Be nice and I'll stop by the office before I quit and pick you up a hot little number." I made kissy lips and winked at him, flipping it back at him.

He blushed. No, he really blushed. He was so cute, my boyish virgin billionaire with his hot man's body. I kissed him on the tip of his nose. Because it was funny and patronizing. And the kind of adorable thing a new wife would do.

He grinned, looking ridiculously happy. Like a new groom, come to think of it. He glanced at the clock. "Shit! Gotta run." He downed his orange juice and grabbed his keys. "We'll talk about your future later."

"Does that mean you don't want me to quit?" I trotted after him as he headed toward the door. "If we need my income...I'm willing to do my part."

"Please do quit, babe. I don't need my friends asking your professional opinion about their underwear. I'll never hear the end of it."

I laughed. "In other words, keep my eyes off their crotches?"

He rolled his eyes. "Yeah, something like that." He grinned.

I grabbed him and gave him a big, long, deep kiss to hold him for the day. Actually, to allay Magda's suspicions. I grabbed the shoulder of the baggy T-shirt he was wearing. "I have to get you out of this shirt."

"One second thought, damn the office," he whispered in a convincing voice. "It can wait." It appeared he'd forgiven me for last night.

And for my part, I was trying to act the role I was supposed to be playing. "No, I mean, really. You can't go out in this ratty old T-shirt and those baggy butt jeans." I grabbed his hand and pulled him toward the bedroom. "I have something better in mind."

Magda turned away. The joke was on her. We weren't going to do the deed.

He followed me like a lamb to the bedroom. Where I closed the door and picked out one of the shirts I'd ordered for him yesterday. "This one. You have to stop dressing in clothes that are too big for you. You have a nice body. Show it off."

He looked me in the eye. "Do I? Have you seen it?"

I cocked an eyebrow. "I've measured it."

He held my gaze as he stripped his shirt off and tossed it on the bed. Crap! His abs were killer. Completely washboard and defined. He looked hard as a rock. I had to keep reminding myself this was Jus.

I grabbed the shirt from the bed and held it out for him to slip into as if I was his valet dressing him. When he'd slid into it, I buttoned it for him. Slowly. Letting my fingers skim his bare skin. He was every bit as rock hard as he looked. I ran my hands over his shoulders, straightening the shirt and feeling him up.

He stood perfectly still, but his breathing became shallow and excited.

I went to his closet and found a sports jacket. "Wear this. You're going to be late."

"We're going to give Magda the wrong idea about my lovemaking skills. She's going to think we had a super quickie." He took the jacket from me.

"It doesn't always need to last hours." I winked at him. "Mad, passionate quickies can sometimes be just what you need." I gave him a gentle shove toward the door. "Get out of here. I'll see you this afternoon."

I saw him to the door and gave him another quick kiss. After he left, I grabbed my phone to check my messages.

I had a text from Lazer. My heart raced.

Where's my picture of you, princess? I can't get anything done without it. I talked to my buddy. You're in! He'll be in touch soon.

I texted him a favorite picture of me. *My hero! Here you go. Can't wait to start!*

An hour and a half later, I'd called in my resignation and was sneaking into my West Seattle apartment, trying to tiptoe past Carl's office. He caught me in the act.

"Kayla! There's the celebrity bride." He came out and gave me an embarrassingly long, tight hug. He finally released me and held me at arm's length, staring me in the eye. "You tightlipped little thing. Married a billionaire over the weekend and didn't let out a peep!" His voice dripped with suspicion. And admiration. Carl, evidently, wasn't against gold-digging women—not on the surface, anyway.

My heart pounded as if it was about to break out of my chest at a run. Carl was one of about two people in the universe who could blow my little charade apart.

"So." He leaned in close again. "What was that big guy and the paper-serving bullshit about yesterday? And playing like you were poor?"

"Oh." I stared at him and forced myself to smile. "Sorry. We were trying to keep things under wraps until we told our family."

"Hmmmm...notifying next of kin first." Carl made it sound like the police notifying family after a murder. "You hadn't told your family? Your mom must be happy about that." He rolled his eyes, totally sarcastic.

Um, crap. I'd stepped in it right out of the box. I fixed a bright smile on my face. "The wedding was...impromptu. In Reno. Calling or texting seemed too impersonal. We were waiting to tell them in person."

Carl cocked an eyebrow, like he didn't believe a word. "You mean you eloped. In Nevada. I thought you said you were away on business? Was that a cover, too? Subterfuge so you could go down there and meet the new boyfriend for the weekend?"

Carl wasn't usually *this* nosy.

I was in a pickle now. "A little of both, actually."

He pursed his lips and shook his head as he made a suspicious grunt in the back of his throat. "So it was unplanned. You both got drunk and got married. That's what I'm hearing."

When did Carl become this sharp?

"The details are unimportant. The main thing is, Jus and I love each other." I laughed, way too nervously. Carl had that effect. He was like a big teddy bear trying to get the truth out of me.

He made thin, serious eyes, and nodded as if deep in thought. "Do you, Kayla? You just broke up with that other guy. Eric. Never liked him. Too full of himself. Didn't like the way he treated you like crap. And made you cry."

"Oh, well. Yeah. Eric." I held up my hands, like what can you do. "He was my biggest mistake. But that's in the past now." I put that dust-my-hands-off tone in my voice. Good riddance!

"On to better and sweeter"—and richer—"guys." I had to stop thinking about Lazer. Last night was like a dream. And a nightmare. I may have met the one just days too late. "Guy. One guy. Obviously." My nervous laugh came out more like a titter. "My husband. You'd love Jus. He's one of the nicest guys around."

Carl was still giving me that suspicious look. "Nice, eh?" Carl was half Canadian, and sometimes that accent came out. "Not the usual way I expect a blushing bride to describe her new hubby."

"You were the one who made the point about Eric being a self-centered douche. I was just making the contrast." I winked.

He didn't look convinced. "Kayla, it's not my business. But you know how much I worry about all my residents. They're like my family. So this is kind of a fatherly warning—be careful. Rebound relationships rarely work. And, you know, there are plenty of girls who want billionaires. Protect your man, is what I'm really saying. I couldn't stand to see you get your heart broken again." The look he gave me was at odds with what he was saying. He didn't look as if he believed I was in love. With Jus, anyway. Maybe with his money.

Just what I needed—belated marital advice from my building manager.

"Sure. About the rent," I said, trying to deflect his attention. "I'll make sure you get it—"

He brushed that point aside. "No need. Your new husband paid a year's rent in advance. His staff took care of it yesterday afternoon."

That was fast. "Yeah, Jus is a sweetie. He likes to take care of me—"

"I was kind of surprised he paid for so long. After seeing the news, I thought you'd be moving in with him and letting the apartment go."

Crap, crap, and double crap! I tried to wave off his suspicions. "Yes, yes, of course. But for now, we haven't made any definite decisions about when we'll move my stuff out. We might need a place to sneak away from the spotlight. You know, a little secret love nest." I winked at Carl as I crossed my fingers that he believed the lie.

"I get you, kiddo." He winked back. "Where are my manners? I should be congratulating you!"

"You congratulate the groom," I said. But I'd landed a billionaire, so maybe I did deserve congratulations.

Carl frowned like he didn't understand my fine point of wedding etiquette.

"You give the bride your best wishes," I prompted.

"Huh. Is that so? Seems kind of like splitting hairs. I don't see the difference. But whatever, best wishes, Kayla!"

"Thank you, Carl. It's been good talking to you." I pointed toward the elevators. "I have to run. I have to pack a few things to move to the penthouse." Gah! That sounded pretentious.

"Sure." He nodded. "Stop by the office before you go and give me a forwarding address. For your mail and packages. And in case I need to get hold of you."

"Will do." I nodded and turned to leave, applauding myself for evading his question about the big paper-serving guy.

"Kayla?"

I stopped and turned back over my shoulder to shoot him a questioning look.

"I'm glad you worked things out with your new husband. However the marriage happened, serving you with divorce papers after a day is pretty shitty."

My mouth fell open. Carl was more astute than I gave him credit for.

"Don't worry. Your secret is safe with me. Them damned media hounds won't get nothing out of me. Not a peep. Hope it works out for you."

"I don't know what you're talking about, Carl. But I appreciate your loyalty."

He nodded. "I get it." He winked, put a finger to his lips, and went back into his office.

I caught the elevator to the third floor, letting out a sigh when the doors closed behind me. That was close!

When I let myself in to my apartment, it looked incredibly small now in comparison to Jus' place. But homey and all mine. And it had actual walls for privacy. There weren't any suspicious housekeepers looking at me as if I was pulling one over on their beloved employer. Just a suspicious building manager. But at least he was loyal to me and kept mostly to his office.

I packed my two largest suitcases full of clothes and things I needed. But there was no way I was stopping by the office to chat more with Carl on the way out. I waited until I saw him leave the building for his morning break and slipped my new address through the slit in his office door on my way out. The car was waiting.

CHAPTER SIX

Justin

When I got to the office, I was mobbed with well wishes and congratulations on both my induction into the Jet City Billionaires' Club and on my surprise nuptials. Flashionista was almost ninety percent women, with a few men mostly concentrated in departments like facilities, transportation, and supplier management. The women were already planning a bridal shower.

Marla, our head buyer, stopped me in the hall and hugged me. "Congrats, Justin! Look at you! Married life is already agreeing with you. You look fabulous. Love the haircut and beard trim."

I rubbed my beard. "Thanks." I'd been getting compliments and double takes all morning. Much more and it would go to my head.

"Cake in the cafeteria. Three o'clock. Don't miss it." She held a finger to her lips. "Shhh. It's a surprise. You didn't hear it from me. Half the girls are heartbroken. Especially now since you're looking so good, bossman!" She winked and ran off to a meeting.

Flashionista had grown quickly this past year, but it was still the friendly, almost family-like atmosphere it had been since the beginning. I used to know everyone by name. We'd outgrown that and gotten too big too fast, but I still recognized most of the faces. And attended a new employees' meeting once a month to meet the newcomers.

Our workforce was mostly under thirty. We had all the hot, fashionable, stylish, trend-spotting girls we could hire. We shot our own daily web catalogues on-site. So we constantly had a stream of attractive models at the offices. Flashionista was a target-rich environment for any guy with a pulse.

It was the brainchild of my business partner, Riggins Thornfield-Smythe, and myself. Riggins was thirty-eight and had already started, and sold, two other highly successful online retail sites. He'd become a billionaire when he sold the majority stake of his previous startup just after we launched Flashionista. And was already a card-carrying member of EIEIO. He'd been out of town last night and unable to make my induction. I expected him back late this evening. He was the main guy I was trying to hide my wedding screw-up from.

When I let myself into my office, there was a large bottle of champagne cooling on my desk and a note of congratulations from Riggins. I should have figured he'd be up on anything to do with the company.

Glad one of us tied the knot. The stability of having a married man at the helm should make Wall Street happy. See you soon. I'm eager to meet the new ball and chain. And surprised she's not one of the Flashion-ista family. Damn, Jus, you couldn't find a girl here?

Good thing he didn't know the circumstances of my marriage. I'd have to tell him that bullshit about Kay being my college crush.

As I dropped my bag next to the champagne, Ophie popped her head into my office. She was the only un-fashionable girl in the entire company. Even our clean-ing ladies, who wore uniforms designed by our staff, were more stylish. I hadn't hired Ophie for her fashion sense.

She was all business this morning, which was unlike her. Not to say she wasn't usually professional. She was generally friendlier. "Harry is here to see you."

I nodded. "Good. Show him in."

She lingered, staring at me with that hurt look in her eyes. "You cut your hair."

I nodded.

She pursed her lips, looking like she wasn't a fan. Like cutting my hair was a betrayal somehow. "*She* made you do it, didn't she?" Her voice was full of scorn and hurt. "She shouldn't be trying to change you, Jus-tin." Her voice cracked a little. "You're perfect the way you are."

I suppose I should have been flattered by her loyalty. She was the only one who thought so. Her crush on me made her blind. She was also the only employee intimate enough with me to say so.

"No." I shook my head and smiled. "I was due for a trim. I needed to look good for my big night."

Her eyes were still narrowed and suspicious. There was an undeniable distance and awkwardness between us now. It was my own damn fault. We were both single nerds. Both driven. Neither of us had dated much or was smooth around the opposite sex.

We worked long hours together. She was safe and easy to talk to. Smart. Efficient. And knew me well. We were bound to grow close and comfortable with each other. I'd fallen into the habit of taking her to networking and office social events. As my assistant. That was my intellectual alibi, anyway. I hadn't meant to lead her on.

Logically, she was a perfect match for me. An attainable match. On a scale of one to ten, we were both fives. That was the way I saw it. Kay was a ten. Way out of my league. If it hadn't been for my money...

If that ID thief hadn't married me in Reno, it was possible Ophie and I would have gotten together. Sooner rather than later. The only thing stopping us was me.

I would have had to reassign her to Riggins. Selfishly, I didn't want to. Not when I relied so heavily on Ophie and enjoyed her company so much. To a guy like me, her attention and adoration were flattering. She got me. I always had the feeling she genuinely liked me for me, not my money. That if I'd been a regular engineer or programmer, she'd still be into me.

My stupidity, and the deception following it, had driven a wedge between us. I couldn't tell her I hadn't set out to hurt her. I hadn't dumped her for a flashy blond on purpose.

"How *was* the induction last night?" she said.

I could see she was trying not to pout and let her hurt show.

I looked her in the eye. "About that, I'm sorry—"

"No, don't be. You didn't have a choice. You had to take your *wife*." How could she put so much snark and derision into that one word? "So? What was it like?"

I still felt like a douche. "Lazer was a showoff." Damn him. "It was at his mountain lodge. He pulled out all the stops."

"Lazer *always* shows off! He can't help himself. It's in his DNA."

Ophie was also the one girl whose head had never been turned by him. "I want all the details. We'll talk later. I'll let Harry in." She turned to go.

"Ophie?"

She stopped and turned with an expectant look on her face.

"Make an appointment for me at the engagement ring store, would you? For today, at one." I felt like a douche and sounded imperious. And unfortunately, I involuntarily smiled at the thought of Kay wearing my ring.

Ophie's face fell. There was the wedge again. I swore the temperature in the room dropped ten degrees. She nodded and showed Harry in. Riggins might be getting a new, highly efficient assistant soon, whether either of us liked it or not.

"How's the newlywed?" Harry shut the office door and whistled. "Look at you! You should get your hair cut more often."

"Shut up. I've gotten so many compliments I'm getting a complex. Did I looked that bad before?"

"Worse." He nodded toward the greater office outside. "There's a boatload of speculation and curiosity about her, about the two of you, about everything, out there."

I nodded. "I know. It's wild."

"They're going to want to meet her." Harry took a seat in the desk chair across from me. "We need to plan something. You need to reassure them your marriage won't adversely affect them. You're the backbone of the company. And there are a lot of girls out there mourning the loss of your bachelorhood."

I laughed. "You're confusing me with Riggins. When he marries, there'll be tears and heartbreak throughout the company. Don't think I don't know he's the hot billionaire around here."

Harry laughed. "He's just the face of the company. Everyone knows your algorithms and vision are what made Flashionista more successful than anything Riggins has done before."

My algorithms were good. But he didn't give Riggins enough credit.

"Invite her to one of our famous afterhours Flashionista cocktail parties and introduce her to the gang there," Harry said. "But be damn sure you've got your story straight and your acting skills up to par first."

Kayla

My car pulled up to the engagement ring store, which is how they were casually known around town, just as Jus did.

Yes, I could drive. Actually loved driving. But I was using the car service because Jus insisted. For my protection. Just until the media buzz from our surprise marriage died down. He hadn't 'fessed up to it, but I was being discreetly followed. I believed he had a security detail following me. All the billionaires did. Lazer had said as much. Because you never know. And, of course, in our case, there was that crazy ID thief to worry about.

Jus claimed Seattle was a good place for billionaires to live. For the most part, the city respected their privacy and left them alone. The world's richest man lived in one of the ritziest suburbs. He had a wife and two kids who lived their lives largely out of the public eye. In fact, you practically never heard about his children. It was as if they didn't exist. His wife was only in the news when she wanted to be. And our famous world's richest man could enjoy his morning coffee in any local Starbucks without being disturbed.

Jus assured me the same would be the case for us, given a little time for the novelty of me to wear off. The city mostly went about its business, used to eccentric people of all types and economic levels.

A crowd of reporters waited for us outside the doors of the store. I laughed inwardly. Of course I'd tipped them off. We needed the press to validate this whacky agreement of ours. We had to be in the public eye and win the public favor in case that identity-stealing-me-impersonator ever showed up and tried to blackmail us.

Plus, and this was key, the jewelry store would absolutely love us for the publicity and prestige we were throwing their way. They would be forever in our debt. If you loved jewelry like I did, this was important. I had my future as the ex Mrs. Green to consider.

Jus jumped from his car, worked his way through the crowd with cameras flashing, and met me as the driver opened the door.

As he took my hand and helped me out, another round of flashes went off. He gave me a questioning look. "How did the press get wind of this?"

I gave him a look like, *Baby, baby, don't be so naïve.*

"You didn't." He grinned.

I winked at him as he pulled me to a stand. "Showtime." I threw my arms around him and kissed him enthusiastically.

As we faced the crowd of reporters hand in hand, they peppered us with questions and comments. "Kayla, how excited *are* you to be getting a ring today?"

I beamed at Jus. "Thrilled, as you can imagine. Not as excited as when Jus proposed. Or when we exchanged vows. But it's no secret—I love my guy." I beamed at him. "And I love jewelry *almost* as much."

The reporter laughed.

One of the women reporters, whom I recognized from the news at five, held a mic out to me. "Is there a particular style you're looking for?"

"I've always been in love with the princess cut." I laughed. "But we'll see!"

"What are you looking for—white gold, gold gold, or platinum? How many carats?"

I laughed again, clutching Jus' arm tightly as I shrugged. "I can't give *everything* away now. All I can really say is I'm eager to see the selection they've pulled together for us."

"We're going to be late," Jus said with a smile. "We have an appointment to keep."

The crowd parted and let us through. I waved to them as Jus opened the first of a pair of double doors for me.

"How are things at the office?" I asked as we stepped inside.

"Crazy, even more than usual. The girls are planning a surprise for me in the cafeteria at three."

I laughed as if he'd said something totally amusing. He held the inner door open for me.

"Really? To congratulate you on your Jet City Billionaire Club membership?"

"Yeah, and our wedding."

"Oh," I said. "Should I make an appearance?"

He shook his head. "That would tip them off I'd found out about the surprise, wouldn't it? No, I think it should be just me this time. No offense, but if you're there, you'll be a distraction." He took a breath. "How did your boss take your resignation?"

"I think she was relieved. The office wants to throw me a bridal shower. Now that I'm married to a billionaire she probably wants to impress me, and you. And see if I can use my connections for their good."

"There's a lot of that wedding shower fever going around." He held the second door open for me.

I touched the back of his head and ran my fingers through his hair where it met his collar. "What does your staff think of your new look? Have you gotten any comments?"

He smiled. "Yeah. I'm going to get a big head. The girls have been ogling me all morning. I've never gotten so many compliments. I'm decently hot now."

"Only decently?"

"All right, smoking. Better?"

"Sure. And not a bit conceited."

The manager met us as we stepped inside. "Welcome, Mr. and Mrs. Green. I'm May. We spoke earlier on the phone," she said to me. "We have a private viewing room reserved for you."

She showed us to a luxurious room in the back of the store and closed the door behind us. Soft classical music played. Crystal chandeliers hung overhead, throwing the light to flatter the trays of diamond rings set out for us to view. Floral arrangements of pink and white roses sat on a table next to a selection of chocolates, cupcakes, petit fours, and tea and coffee.

The room even smelled expensive, like tasteful, elegant perfume. A guard stood at the door.

"Taking your preferences into consideration, I've pulled a selection of rings I hope will meet your expectations," May said. "If you don't see anything you like, I'll be more than happy to pull more."

I nodded. "Thank you." I turned to Jus. "When we spoke earlier, I let her know the styles I prefer."

She didn't patronize us with the usual speech on the four Cs of diamonds. She simply pointed to the trays of rings and the refreshments. "Please. Help yourself. Browse as you like. I'm here to answer any questions. Take your time. There's no rush."

Jus and I were still holding hands. "How much are you thinking of spending?" I whispered to him. "A good starting recommendation is one month's salary," I teased. "But anywhere between one and three is good. I'm easy. One month is fine with me. How much is one twelfth of a billion?"

He laughed. "Eighty-three point three three million."

"You know that off the top of your head?" I asked. Had he been expecting that question?"

"I'm good with math in my head."

Genius, more like.

"FYI, I have more than one billion. In net assets." He leaned into me and whispered in that deep, sexy voice of his that was still startling to hear, "Don't get any ideas. A deal's a deal."

Oh, darn. I wasn't going to get another twelfth of a billion out of him in the form of a ring.

"Going with the salary thing isn't to your advantage," he said. "I take a small, really small salary. Based on that—"

"Shut up!" I squeezed his hand. "There's no way I'd wear any eighty-three-million-dollar ring on my finger anyway. Do they even make rings that expensive? Can you imagine? I'd be a ready target for someone to rob and hit me over the head with a lead pipe to get my ring. I have no intention of dying because I'm wearing your ring."

He smiled. "Good. We're on the same page."

He stopped by the dessert table and grabbed a chocolate. I was too excited to eat anything. We wandered around, looking at trays of rings. They were all gorgeous. And obviously expensive.

Jus didn't know that when I talked to May earlier, I asked her not to show us anything over twenty-five thousand. Yeah, I wasn't out to get his billions. The rings she'd selected were all gorgeous. I stopped in front of a tray that caught my eye and tried a few on.

Maybe it was gauche, but Jus asked the natural question. A guy had a right to know how much he was spending. "What do these start at?"

"Twenty thousand." May looked apologetic, but her eyes leaped with hope. Maybe Jus would be up for spending more than my limit. "We can order out for more expensive rings if you like. Or design something custom—"

I shook my head. "These are perfect. I don't need more."

Jus grinned at me, egging me on. "Money's no object. Up to a point. I was thinking of spending more like a hundred thousand."

I shook my head. "I'm not going around with the equivalent of a small house on my finger. As I said, I don't want someone bashing me over the head for my jewelry."

"What kind of neighborhoods are you planning to go to?" he teased.

I rolled my eyes.

"I'll keep you safe." He grabbed my hand and squeezed it.

"My hero!" I laughed.

"Babe, do you want people thinking I'm cheap?" He was playing devoted groom too well. "My love for you knows no limits. Especially not dollar limits."

He was such a tease.

"I don't *care* if they think you're cheap. I want them to see that I didn't marry you for your money." After being accused of that all day long, not looking mercenary was becoming increasingly important to me. I'm sure it sounded desperately romantic to anyone who overheard. "I married you for you."

I looked deep into his eyes, really putting it on. "I love *you*. Not your money." Maybe I could fool at least one innocent bystander.

Even though she stood to lose out on a bigger commission, May got teary-eyed. Gullible, but I liked her for that.

Jus grinned and gave me a quick kiss. "I love you, too."

I smiled back at him, thinking he understood. "The average guy spends about four thousand on a wedding set. Five or six times as much as that should be sufficient. That's the price of a small car. And the most almost any groom spends. That's way more than I need."

"Kay," he said. "I hate to point this out, but you could just as easily be hit over the head for a small car."

"I thought you were keeping me safe?"

He laughed and kissed me again. I was actually enjoying myself. After debating for less than half an hour, I picked a set that outshone any of my married friends' rings. And was, quite frankly, the ring of my dreams. I'd been to enough weddings in the last four years to know.

May promised to have it sized and sent by courier to us Thursday morning. "Would you like the engagement ring soldered to the wedding band?"

I opted not to. "No. I think there will be times when I'll want to just wear the simple diamond band."

She turned her attention to Jus' ring, looking me in the eye. "How much would you like to spend on the groom's ring?"

Oh, crap. That was part of the deal—the bride bought the groom's ring. And I had no money. If I told her a couple hundred, would she laugh me out of the store?

Jus came to my rescue. "A simple gold band is all I want."

She measured his ring size and called for another tray, this time of men's rings. Jus picked his. "Add it to my tab." He pulled out his credit card and handed it over before I could protest. He seemed practiced at picking up the tab over others' protests. Probably mostly feeble protests, as mine was.

I pulled May aside and asked her to share a picture of my ring and the specs with the waiting press.

And then we were done. The cars were waiting for us when we stepped out of the store. I relaxed on the way home, eager to get back to the penthouse and collapse. I'd had enough stress for one day. Enough pretending to be in love with a guy I barely knew. Enough being on my guard, smiling for cameras, and having flashes go off in my face. Enough of not being who I really was. Of my life being a play lived out in the real world. Enough of blending into Jus' life while putting mine on hold. I just wanted to kick back, be myself, and decompress.

I let myself into the penthouse and tossed my purse on the console table before kicking off my shoes. I was looking around for Magda when I spotted a dark-haired woman sitting in a chair with her back to me. There was something familiar about her.

"May I help you?" I said.

She spun around and I knew immediately who she had to be. My heart dove for my stomach and my smile wobbled.

"Diana Green. Justin's mom." Her words were like ice. "We need to talk."

Gina Robinson is the award-winning author of the contemporary new adult romances *Rushed, Crushed, Reckless Longing, Reckless Secrets,* and *Reckless Together* and the Agent Ex series of humorous romantic suspense novels. She's currently working on the next installment of Switched at Marriage.

Connect with Gina Online:

My Website: http://www.ginarobinson.com/
Twitter: @ginamrobinson
Facebook: www.facebook.com/GinaRobinsonAuthor

www.ingramcontent.com/pod-product-compliance
Lightning Source LLC
Chambersburg PA
CBHW060644130626
46555CB00002B/944